SAY YES SUMMER

Lindsey Roth Culli

Delacorte Press

Produced by Alloy Entertainment

Text copyright © 2020 by Alloy Entertainment
Front jacket photograph copyright © 2020 by Kimberly Genevieve/Gallery Stock
Back jacket photograph copyright © 2020 by Joel Redman/Gallery Stock

All rights reserved. Published in the United States by Delacorte Press, an imprint of Random House Children's Books, a division of Penguin Random House LLC, New York.

Delacorte Press is a registered trademark and the colophon is a trademark of Penguin Random House LLC.

GetUnderlined.com

Educators and librarians, for a variety of teaching tools, visit us at RHTeachersLibrarians.com

Library of Congress Cataloging-in-Publication Data
Names: Culli, Lindsey Roth, author.
Title: Say yes summer / Lindsey Roth Culli.
Description: First edition. | New York : Delacorte Press, [2020] | Summary: Before heading off to college in the fall, Rachel Walls decides to give in to the universe for the summer and say yes to everything, bringing her friendship, new experiences, and, if she lets her guard down, love.
Identifiers: LCCN 2019022445 | ISBN 978-0-399-55231-1 (hardcover) | ISBN 978-0-399-55233-5 (ebook)
Subjects: CYAC: Change—Fiction. | Courage—Fiction. | Friendship—Fiction. | Dating (Social customs)—Fiction. | Summer—Fiction.
Classification: LCC PZ7.1.C835 Say 2020 | DDC [Fic]—dc23

The text of this book is set in 11-point Adobe Garamond Pro.
Interior design by Cathy Bobak

Printed in the United States of America
10 9 8 7 6 5 4 3 2 1
First Edition

For Sam. Always.

1

The middle of delivering your valedictorian speech is a terrible time to have an existential crisis.

"I, uh . . ." I glance down at the damp, wrinkly index card clenched in my hand, my meticulously typed notes blurring together until they look more like alphabet soup than the speech I've spent every available moment of the last month perfecting—skipping my lunch period to work on my draft in the library, revising in my head in the shower at night, chanting the words over and over as I sprinkled shredded mozzarella on pizzas in the steamy kitchen at my parents' restaurant. I can feel my cheeks heating now as sure as if I'm standing directly in front of the five-hundred-degree oven, a salty band of sweat beading on my upper lip.

I force my eyes up at the crowd in the auditorium, my classmates gazing back at me with a mixture of boredom and what I'm pretty sure is grim anticipation, all of them wondering if I might be about to choke and go rushing off the stage: Tricia Whitman, whom I know from her many #cruiseclothes Instagram posts, is spending the next two weeks on a luxury ocean liner somewhere in the Caribbean. Henry Singh, who had a huge fight with his boyfriend in the middle of the diner a couple weeks ago and dumped an entire Caesar salad onto the guy's lap before storming out into the parking lot. Cecily Johnston, the only person at our whole school who scored higher than me on the SAT.

I'm not friends with any of these people, to be absolutely clear. The truth is I've never even talked to most of them. But that doesn't mean I don't know what they're like, even if the vast majority of them probably saw my name in the program this morning, turned to their neighbor, and said something along the lines of *Who the hell is Rachel Walls?*

I wince at the thought of it, imagining their furrowed brows as they tried unsuccessfully to place me: Was I that foreign exchange student who was only here for one semester, maybe? The weird theater girl who always wore shapeless black dresses and a netted veil? An unexpectedly brilliant janitor who snuck into Ms. Ali's math room late at night to do complicated calc proofs on the whiteboard?

Then, vague recognition slowly dawning as I stepped up to the podium: *Oh . . . her.*

The gunner. The wet blanket. The prude.

Get a grip, Patatina. I hear Nonna's voice inside my head in the instant before I finally spot her with my mom and stepdad near the back of the auditorium, her neat gray bob cocked slightly to the side as she waits for me to continue. I take a deep breath, getting a lungful of forced air and perfume and polyester-graduation-robe BO for my trouble, then clear my throat one more time. After all, just because I'm not exactly about to be voted most popular in the yearbook—that would be Clayton Carville, he of Westfield soccer stardom and a criminally beautiful jawline—doesn't mean I haven't earned this. The opposite, actually. In fact, the choices that have rendered me utterly invisible to these people are the very same ones that have led me here, to this moment and what comes next.

That is, delivering this damn speech and then getting the hell out of town so that my real life can finally start.

Pressing my hands against the lectern, I continue. "If you go out to Oval Beach today and build a sand castle, then go back tomorrow, you'll find it washed away. That movement toward chaos—in science it's known as *entropy*—is inevitable. Nothing escapes its relentlessness. In a closed system, left to its own devices, disorder or chaos always increases. Always.

"Order, then, requires effort. Energy. Boatloads of it. And our successes here at Westfield have been no exception. Debate clubs like ours don't make it to the National Tournament without practice. Soccer teams like ours don't win the State Championships without collaboration and teamwork." I glance at Clayton here— and okay, it's possible I added the soccer line specifically so I would have an excuse to look at him, sprawled in the second row with his long legs slightly spread—before continuing.

"Fellow graduates, we didn't get here because of randomness.

We're here today because of hard work. Because of diligence. Because we expended energy and made sacrifices. And while the accomplishments of the last few years should be celebrated, this is called a *commencement* ceremony. Commence, as in 'to begin.' Today we mark the ending of high school *and* the beginning of something new."

I glance up at Clayton again, my gaze drawn to his lithe, lanky figure even without the benefit of a handy contextual excuse, and almost drop my notecards altogether when I realize he's looking back at me. Which, fine, yes, intellectually I know that makes sense—after all, I'm actively delivering his high school graduation speech—but then he *grins,* all dimples and mischievous expression, the split-second catch of his tongue between his straight white teeth.

Can you get pregnant from a smile? Asking for myself.

It's not until Principal Howard steps forward, says something into the mic, and the entire auditorium erupts in cheers that I figure out I must somehow have finished talking. Out in the audience everyone stands, takes off their caps, and throws them into the air. Not me, though. Frankly, my hand-eye coordination is nothing to brag about even when I *haven't* just immaculately conceived Clayton Carville's smile-baby. There's no way I'm about to risk it now. Watch it land six rows away, leaving me stuck with somebody else's cap—and sweat, and hair product, and dandruff.

Gross.

Instead I tuck the thing beneath my arm and clap politely, returning a few random high fives before I start to make my way through the thick, noisy crowd. I've just spotted the back of my stepdad's head—he's got a bald spot there he keeps trying to cover up by combing his hair all different ways, but the truth is he isn't fooling anybody—when Ruoxi grabs my arm.

"Rachel!" She's holding her cap, too, which probably explains a lot about why exactly she's my best friend. She's also technically my *only* friend—unless you count Miles, which I emphatically do not. This doesn't change the fact that other than Nonna, she's basically my favorite person on the face of the planet. I have no idea what I'm going to do without her this summer—or, for that matter, at Northwestern in the fall. "Good job, lady."

"Thaaaank you." I bend down to wrap my arms around her short, slight frame. "And thank you for not passing out from boredom even though you'd already heard the whole thing ten thousand times."

"It got better with repetition," she says, scooping her thick, wavy hair off the back of her neck and fanning herself a little. Even in her cork-heeled sandals, she's a full head shorter than me, her hot-pink toenails bright against her dark skin. "Like a Justin Bieber song."

"That's me and the Biebs," I tell her. "Shaping young minds. Inspiring the youths."

"Exactly." Ruoxi takes a step closer, casting a dirty look over her shoulder as some lax bro jostles her from behind. "So, here's a thing that happened," she says, lowering her voice. "I was sitting next to Paul Haberman during the ceremony, right?"

"Can I ask you a question?" I blurt out, thinking back on my midspeech meltdown. Paul Haberman writes for the *Westfield Courier* and got a ton of followers on Snapchat by posting these weirdly artful photos of his cafeteria lunch every single day for a year; as far as the socioeconomic ladder of popularity goes, I'd call him solidly middle class. "Did he have any idea who I was? Like, when I got up there, I mean?"

"What?" Ruoxi looks at me oddly. "I don't know. I didn't ask him. Why wouldn't he?"

"Forget it." I shake my head. Best friends or not, *I spent the last four years purposely cultivating total anonymity and this morning I started worrying that might have been a strategic misstep* is not a conversation for this particular moment. "Sorry. Continue."

"Okaaaay?" Ruoxi isn't convinced, but she doesn't push it. "Anyway, Paul asked what I was doing tonight and when I said probably hanging out with you, he said Bethany's doing a thing at her house and we should come."

I bark a laugh in the moment before I realize she isn't kidding. "Wait," I protest, *"really?"* Bethany has been dating Clayton on and off since sophomore year; the back of her house is directly across a narrow creek from the back of mine, which means I've had a front-row view of their various breakups and makeups—and, okay, makeouts—for just about that long. Not that I make a habit of spying on them or anything, but I have eyeballs, and a conveniently located bedroom window, and honestly I am in my pajamas by eleven p.m. most Saturday nights. Things happen. "You want to go?"

"Not with that tone in your voice I don't," Ruoxi says pointedly.

Then she shrugs. "But yeah, kind of. I don't know. It could be fun, right?"

"I mean, if you want to get your stomach pumped and catch HPV, yeah, it sounds like a blast."

"Oh, come on, Rach." Ruoxi frowns. "Do you honestly think it's like that?"

"Yes," I say flatly. I may not be a connoisseur of high school parties, but I've crept on enough people's social media—and seen enough *Friday Night Lights*—to know exactly what we'd be getting into if we went over to Bethany's tonight. I can stand awkwardly alone in a corner in the comfort of my own home, thank you. I don't need to put on eyeliner and go do it in public. "I think it is exactly like that."

"Well, fine," Ruoxi says, apparently unbothered. "Maybe it really is like that. But I leave for Interlochen tomorrow, you know? And it's going to be so intense and high pressure and . . . I don't know. Don't you ever get curious? About, like . . ." She trails off.

"Being a normal person?" I supply.

"Kind of!" Ruoxi laughs a little, though I don't think either one of us actually finds it particularly funny. "School's over, you know? We did it. And it's only one night."

She's serious, I realize, feeling a tiny pang of guilt for how bitchily I dismissed the idea. After all, it's not like I don't understand her impulse. Wasn't I literally just having a fairly major freak-out about this exact thing? "You're right," I tell her, mustering a smile. "You should totally go."

"And you should come with me," she says immediately. "You know who will be there, right?" She smirks. "That was a very slick and organic soccer team shout-out in your speech today, PS."

"Thank you." For one truly bonkers moment, I actually consider it: obsessing over my outfit and wasting an hour in front of a YouTube tutorial trying unsuccessfully to figure out how to make my hair look like Bethany's, drinking enough beer to forget myself for a little while. But in the end, just like always, I shake my head. "I actually really can't," I lie. "I'm on the schedule at the restaurant tonight."

"Oh, nice try." Ruoxi purses her bright red lips. "You're telling me your parents are honestly going to make you spend graduation night slinging pizzas?"

Of course they're not. In fact, they'd probably fall over dead of happiness if I said I wanted to go to an actual party, to socialize with my actual peers. Hell, they'd probably offer to pay for a keg. "Yeeees?" I try.

Ruoxi rolls her eyes. "You have your entire life to work," she reminds me, swatting me gently on the arm with her graduation cap. "This summer you should try to play. Just a little."

I make a face. "Oh, okay, Ms. I'm-going-to-fancy-pants-camp-where-I'll-be-practicing-piano-twenty-four-hours-a-day."

"And wearing knee socks with shorts." Ruoxi groans. "Don't forget about the knee socks with shorts." She's smiling, though. I know she's actually thrilled about her summer prospects, ugly uniform and all. "To be fair, I think it's only like twenty-three hours and fifteen minutes of the day. There are breaks to eat wholesome food and use the bathroom."

"Assuming you go quickly and don't talk to anyone while you're in there."

"Exactly." Ruoxi smiles. "Text me if you change your mind about tonight, okay?"

That . . . is definitely not going to happen, but it doesn't feel like it's worth it to say so. Over Ruoxi's shoulder, I can see my family waiting by the auditorium doors, my parents with identical goofy smiles and my little brother Jackson playing a game on his phone. Nonna waves both arms, bracelets jangling like she's trying to land a 747.

"I will," I promise, and hug Ruoxi one more time. I edge through a row of red velvet seats toward the exit, swearing under my breath as my plasticky robe snags on a scarred wooden armrest. I've just pulled myself free when someone says my name.

"Hmm?" I look up and freeze where I am, like I've stepped in a giant wad of gum: Standing in the row of seats directly behind me is Clayton Carville himself, his robe unzipped to reveal navy blue khakis and a starchy white dress shirt. He's undone the top button and loosened his tie so I can see the hollow of his throat beneath his Adam's apple, where the skin is thin and vulnerable-looking. "Nice speech today," he says.

Holy crap. "You too!" I say automatically, then wince. "I mean . . . um . . . Congratulations. On . . . graduating." *Real smooth, Rachel. Truly, brilliant work.*

"Thanks," Clayton says, ducking his head almost shyly, scrubbing a hand through his close-cropped hair. "Anyway. I'll see you around, I guess?"

"Sure!" I chirp, though truthfully I have no idea where or when *around* might be. He's headed to Marquette in the fall, I've deduced from the hoodie he started wearing to school after spring break, but other than that I don't know anything about his future except for the fact that this is the point where it diverges from mine, two-roads-in-a-yellow-wood style. I was never brave enough to tell Clayton how I feel about him. I was never brave enough to talk to Clayton, period, and now it's too late. "Um. Take care of yourself."

"I will," Clayton says, and there's that smile again, quick and generous. It's the smile of a person who has never obsessed over whether or not to go to a party. It's the smile of a person who has never worried that possibly he did the first seventeen years of his life completely wrong. "Bye, Rach."

"Yo, Clayton!" somebody hollers from across the auditorium; he's gone before I can even register the nickname, or how easily it seemed to come out of his mouth. I don't know how long I stand there before finally coming back to myself—making my way across the auditorium toward my family, glancing over my shoulder for one last look.

2

*B*ack at home, I change out of my graduation robe and into leggings and a hoodie, scooping my hair into a topknot before thundering back down the stairs into the kitchen. "There's our girl," my stepdad says, looking up from the crossword in the daily local paper. He's sitting at the table next to a pile of Walls family detritus: this week's Meijer circular and a couple of abandoned water glasses and my financial aid packet from Northwestern, Jackson's baseball glove balanced on top of a stack of overdue library books. "Here's one for you. 'Precollege, for short.' Four letters, maybe starts with *E*."

I pluck a grape from the slightly withered bunch on the counter, considering. "Elhi," I finally say.

He whispers the word back to himself and writes it in. "Huh."

"Hey, someone grab this, please." Mom clambers through the back door, the screen door slamming behind her with a *thwack*. She drops a kiss on my forehead, then sets two massive, grease-spotted pizza boxes down on the counter. One of the perks of owning a fast-casual Italian restaurant: all the pizza we could ever want.

And also a bunch we don't.

"I just keep replaying your speech in my head," she tells me, peeling a plastic grocery bag off her wrist and pulling a package of *Congrats, Grad!* plates from its crinkly depths along with a matching set of napkins. "Seriously, Ma, have you ever heard a more brilliant graduation speech in your entire life?"

"Never," Nonna chimes in from her spot on the flowered sofa in the living room, her tone brooking even fewer arguments than usual. "She was stunning."

"We are so proud of you," Mom continues, taking my face in both palms. Her hands are rough, with the ragged cuticles of a person who doesn't have time or patience for things like manicures. Her forearms are speckled with burns from the oven at the restaurant. "*I* am so proud. So very, very proud." Tears begin to prick at the corners of my eyes, and Mom's quivering lip tells me she's feeling the same.

"Uh-oh," Nonna says, hauling herself up off the sofa with a quiet groan before encircling both of us in a hug. "Here come the waterworks." She smells like juniper and talcum, familiar; as she wraps us up in her surprisingly strong arms, I can't help but think about how, as hard as I've been working to get into college and out of here, I am going to be so, so sad to leave.

"All right, enough," Mom says finally—the first to break away, blotting the corners of her eyes with one businesslike thumb. "Pizza's getting cold."

"Pizza's already cold," Jackson points out, scampering into the kitchen in his cargo shorts and tube socks, hair somehow sticking up in every direction even though I know for a fact Dad made him gel it down for the ceremony earlier. My brother is twelve, and he really excels at it. "That's the sad truth of other people's garbage pizza."

"Easy, you," Dad says, peeling the cellophane off the paper plates and dealing them like a deck of cards before lifting the lid on the pizza box, the smell of the garlic butter we brush on all our crusts filling the kitchen. This particular garbage pie is pepperoni, black olives, banana peppers, and . . . Ugh.

"Is that pineapple?" I can't help but ask.

Mom shrugs. "Can't let screwups go to waste, even on graduation day. You can just pick it off."

False. Unlike some other toppings, pineapple has juice, and you cannot pick that off.

I briefly consider investigating the second box before deciding whatever is in there is probably worse than pineapple and settling on the slice that's been least violated by hunks of brightly colored tropical fruit. I push a stack of vendor invoices out of the way and take a seat at the table as Nonna gets herself a can of lemon-lime seltzer from the fridge—the store brand, which she insists is her favorite—and sidles up next to me.

"So," she says, "tell me again why you're still here?"

I give her a weird look. "College doesn't actually start until the fall, you realize."

"Yes, thank you. I haven't completely lost my faculties." She thwaps me over the head with the pack of napkins before opening it and handing me one.

"'The terrible and the great,'" Dad pipes up from across the table. "Five letters. Third letter is an *a*." It's not a question, but he's waiting for an answer. The two of us have been doing the crossword together for as long as I can remember; it was one of the things we bonded over when he and my mom got married. When I'm quiet now, he looks up. "What. Don't tell me you graduated six hours ago and you've already forgotten everything you learned."

"Somehow, I think I missed Crosswords 101." I pop a banana pepper into my mouth, thinking. "Tsars," I announce once I've swallowed, grinning at him from across the table. "As in Ivan and Peter."

Nonna blinks at me in confusion.

"Ivan the Terrible and Peter the Great?" I say.

"See? She's stunning." Nonna kisses my forehead the same way Mom did a few minutes ago. "Who else needs pizza?" she asks before setting a plate in front of my dad, who's still lost in his own intricately gridded world. He absently picks up the slice and takes a bite, crust first.

"So?" Nonna prods again, sitting down beside me with her own slice—the second box was sausage and mushroom, I realize now, which I would have figured out if I'd bothered to look for myself. "About that party."

I shake my head. "You sound like Ruoxi."

"Ru's at the party?" Nonna's eyebrows rise. "And you're not?"

"There is no party!" I lie.

"Leave her alone," Mom says, waving her hand in the air. One thing I've always appreciated about my mom is that—unlike almost everyone else in my life—she's never once nagged me about *stepping outside my comfort zone!* or *just taking a chance every once in a while!* She of all people totally gets it: how one false move might lead you down a path you can't turn back from. How one mistake might alter the entire course of your life. After all, it happened to her, though she's never put it quite so baldly. Still, it's not a secret that I was born in what would have been her freshman year of college, or that until she met Jim she was a single mom trying to raise me on waitressing tips.

She was impulsive—just once, she didn't think before she acted. And she paid for it.

"Even if there was a party, I wouldn't be going," I say now, swallowing the rest of my pizza crust before getting up and trashing my paper plate. I grab a seltzer of my own, holding it up in a salute before heading for the staircase. "I've got a hot date tonight"—I see the excitement flash across Nonna's face—"with a book."

"How completely on brand," she says. "This she got from your side." Nonna tsks at Dad, whose nose is still buried in his crossword.

She's chiding him, ostensibly, but the truth is I know they both like the thought that he could pass something on to me, genes be damned.

"'Bois de Boulogne, par example,'" Dad calls as I'm heading up the stairs to my bedroom. "Four letters. Ends with a *c.*"

"Don't look at me," Mom says. "I speak Italian, not French."

"Parc," I call back into the kitchen. Nonna's laughter is the last thing I hear before I shut my bedroom door.

✳

I meant what I said to Nonna—I'm fully intending to spend this summer catching up on all the non-school reading I've put aside over the course of the last four years—but I can barely concentrate for sounds of Bethany's party drifting in through the open window: The thumping bass of a Beyoncé song. A splash as someone cannonballs into the water. A girl laughing as loudly as if she were sitting right here on my bed.

I roll over on the mattress and rest my arms on the windowsill, peering out into the deep blue darkness. It's that lovely temperature between warm and cool, the last dregs of the heat of the day still lingering in the air. I can smell honeysuckle mixed in with the brackish scent of the narrow, rocky creek that runs along the property line behind our house. I breathe in, watching as a couple of kids careen down Bethany's dock before stopping short right at the edge. The two of them collapse with laughter, coming precariously close to ending up in the water anyway. They lie there for a while, looking up at the stars, and I watch as they eventually roll toward each other and start to kiss.

Reckless, I think, knowing even as the word occurs to me that I sound even older—and definitely crustier—than Nonna. To be honest, I'm not even sure if it's the running or the kissing that seems so risky and ill-advised.

I look away just in time to spy another pair standing in the distance, their dark outlines just barely visible through a copse of pine trees on the opposite shore: Clayton and Bethany, I realize immediately, leaning forward in spite of myself.

It's probably creepy that I'd know Clayton's stance anywhere, the shape of his body obvious to me from a hundred yards away, though I like to think it's simply a testament to my keen powers of observation and commitment to best research practices. Still, the cold fact remains that until today, Clayton and I had had exactly three substantial interactions over the course of our high school careers, none of which were exactly what you'd call romantically promising. Behold, *Rachel and Clayton's Greatest Hits:*

Freshman year, we had geometry with Mr. Rosen, a sadist who wore an army-green pair of TOMS shoes every day even in winter and liked to make us race proofs against each other up at the front of the room. I was up against Victoria Ahmed, thought I'd won, and was fully preparing to take my victory lap when I realized that what I'd *actually* done was write "Clayton property of multiplication" instead of "Com-mutative property of multiplication" in eight-inch letters on the whiteboard.

Sophomore year, I was picking up a fresh-packed pint of ice cream for my mom at Moxie's in town and ran into him getting sundaes with his family—including his Tory Burch–clad mother, who leaned close to my ear and politely informed me that my skirt was tucked into my underwear. Clayton had no comment at that time.

Senior year I swung by the chemistry lab during my free period to return an AP study guide I'd borrowed from Mrs. Lee—and walked in on Bethany and Clayton in full-on makeout mode. Three months later and the image is still burned into my retinas: Bethany boosted up onto the edge of one of the counter-height benches with Clayton standing snugly between her legs, his elegant hands creeping up her denim-covered thighs. They were going at it so enthusiasti-cally that I probably could have escaped without either one of them noticing, except for the part where I was so surprised I knocked over an entire cart of beakers, which shattered all over the linoleum floor with a sound like the explosion at freaking Chernobyl.

Tonight the two of them stand facing each other by the water's edge, not getting closer but not apart, either. Bethany leans in for a second—a kiss, maybe?—but it's hard to tell. I shift up onto my knees on the mattress, squinting through the screen for a closer look and wishing idly for a pair of binoculars, although to be fair that would be over the line even for me. Whatever happens, it only lasts the briefest of moments before she steps back again, moving farther away from him than where she started. Holy crap, are they having a fight? It wouldn't be the first time I've caught them melting down from my perch in the crow's nest of my bedroom. One time last summer she pushed him right into the creek.

After a moment Bethany shakes her head and turns back in the direction of the house, hands shoved into the pockets of her perfectly shredded cutoffs. I'm expecting Clayton to follow, but instead he dawdles by the creek, reaching down and trailing his fingers along the ground for a moment before coming up with a couple of stones and tossing them into the water with audible plunks. Just then, his head moves as though he's glancing up toward my window. Toward me.

My breath catches in my throat, a flare of panic before I remember that at least he can't see me.

Wait. *Can* he see me?

That's when Clayton raises a hand and waves.

Oh my God. He can see me.

I face-plant into my pillows, letting out a muffled, horrified wail. I might actually be dying. Yep, I'm dead.

I slither out of bed and army-crawl over to the light switch, reaching up and standing for a split second before I turn it off. When I get up the courage to sneak a glance outside again, this time under the cover of darkness, Bethany's side of the creek is empty and deserted.

The party behind it rages on.

3

Ruoxi forbade me from going over to say goodbye because she's heading out so early, which doesn't stop me from hauling myself out of bed in the blue summer dawn and showing up at her front door with a London Fog—her favorite drink from Ground Up, which opens at six every morning to catch the beach jogger crowd.

I hand her the cup and take note of her smudgy eye makeup, bedhead, and the slight green pallor to her normally dewy cheeks. "So I take it you had a good time?" I tease.

Ruoxi sinks down on the front steps of her parents' house instead of answering, easing the lid off her London Fog and taking a tentative sip. "Oh my God," she moans, setting it down on the concrete beside her and burying her face in her knees. "Why is it so *bright* out?"

The sun is just barely peeking up over the edge of the lake, actually, but this doesn't feel like the right moment to state the obvious. After a moment, Ruoxi hauls herself upright again, then immediately lets out a loud, wet-sounding belch. "Oh my God," she says again, clapping a hand over her mouth. "I'm a monster. I am so sorry." She offers me a sleepy smile. "Anyway, it was fun. There were like a hundred people there—including, as predicted, your boyfriend."

I shake my head, leaving out the part where after last night he's probably out filing a restraining order against me at this very moment. "He's not my boyfriend," I remind her. "He's not my anything, actually."

"Uh-huh." Her eyes dart to me. "Carrie was there too."

I'm quiet for a minute, the mention of Carrie's name hitting me with the same weird pang of loneliness and regret it always does. "Oh," I say finally. All through middle school, Carrie was the third leg of our tidy little equilateral triangle, the three of us completely inseparable until we got to ninth grade and everything changed. Or, more accurately: Carrie changed. "I mean, that makes sense, right? She and Bethany are, like, obsessed with each other."

"Are they still?" Ruoxi asks, running her thumb over the lid of her coffee cup. "They weren't really hanging out last night at all. Carrie was kind of keeping to herself, actually."

"Huh." I file that piece of information away for later. "Did you guys talk?" I ask. I don't know if I'm hoping they did or they didn't.

"Not really," Ruoxi said. "Just hi and bye and stuff, although I will say she didn't seem as overtly bitchy as I remember her being. Maybe we're all mellowing with age." She shrugs. "You totally should've come."

"Oh, I don't know," I tease, rattling the ice in my cup. "I kind of feel like I got the full experience here."

"And none of the regret," Ruoxi admits, letting out another quiet burp.

I help her pack the rest of her things and bring them out to the car, waving to her parents before hugging her goodbye. Cell phones aren't really allowed at Interlochen, but we make a pact to text each other as often as we can. Except for a few days after she gets back from camp, this is the last time we'll really be together before college starts, and I can tell we're both feeling wobbly. "Seriously, though," she says, even as her dad points impatiently to his watch from the driver's seat, "try to have some fun this summer, okay?"

"Sorting silverware and waiting tables count?" I ask.

"It does not, in fact." She frowns. "When I get back, I expect to be fully regaled with all the tales of your adventures."

"Swashbuckling and sword fighting, then," I tease. "Got it."

Ruoxi doesn't laugh. "I'm serious, Rach," she says. "You deserve it. If not now, then when, right?"

"Right," I echo, though the truth is my skin is prickling unpleasantly. I can't get over the sneaking sense that she got drunk at one party and now she thinks she's some kind of authority on living a wild and carefree life. After all, this is *Ruoxi,* who skipped the prom

not three weeks ago so that she could practice Chopin's Etude in G#
Minor for the seven hundredth time. Is she really about to tell me I
need to loosen up?

And—ugh, why is this becoming the theme of my life all of a
sudden—is it possible she's right?

"Be good," I tell her finally, hugging her tightly in the early-
morning sunshine. She waves out the window of the car as she goes.

✳

"Two Gondolas," my dad calls over his shoulder into the kitchen
at the restaurant that afternoon, soft rock piping in over the stereo
and a huge pot of red sauce bubbling away on the industrial range.
"One pig, one chicken. And can somebody check on that order of
mozzarella sticks?"

I glance at the clock on the wall above the register. *Seventy-seven
days, eighteen hours, and twenty-two*—twenty-one—*minutes.*

That's all the time I have left *before.*

Before I leave for Northwestern. Before my life can really start.

It's all so close I can *feel* it.

For now, though, I get started on the sandwiches, listening with
one ear as Lionel Richie croons in the background. Gondolas are
basically glorified subs stuffed with cold cuts, provolone cheese, a
couple mealy hydroponic tomato slices, and a handful of lettuce;
really the only thing Italian about them is the fact that they're made
on loaves of Nonna's freshly baked bread, which doesn't change the

fact that they've given our humble family restaurant a kind of cult following. It's a lot of food for five bucks, I guess.

I slice one sandwich in half and stick our trademark mini-pickle-on-an-Italian-flag-toothpick in each half before setting the red-and-white paper boats in the window. "Order up!" I call just as Miles finally shuffles in through the back door to the kitchen, grabbing his apron off the hook and squashing his DiPasquale's baseball cap down over his tangle of dark, curly hair.

"About time," I tell him, nodding with my chin at the deep fryer. "I thought I was going to be stuck back here covering for you all afternoon."

"Sorry," he says, lifting the basket out of the hot oil and dumping the mozzarella sticks onto a plate. "Got held up."

"Uh-huh." I brush some stray lettuce off my station. "Doing what, exactly?"

Miles looks at me sideways as he ladles a cup of marinara into a plastic ramekin, his olivey face all suggestion. "You really want to know?"

I roll my eyes. "Don't be gross."

"I didn't say anything!" he defends himself. "If your mind's in the gutter, that's between you and the Lord." Then he grins at me, revealing one crooked canine tooth. "Hey, decent speech yesterday."

"Uh, thanks," I say, waiting for the inevitable punch line of whatever joke he's setting up and raising an eyebrow when it doesn't come. In fact, this is the closest to genuine I've heard him possibly ever, which is saying something. Miles and I literally grew up together;

our grandparents were old family friends, and when my birth dad (or, as I like to refer to him, my genetic donor) took off, Miles's mom insisted we stay in the apartment above their garage for a few months while my mom got her act together. *A few months* turned into four years, during which time there was ample opportunity for Nonna to snap a million blurry pictures of us in the bath together, a fact Miles loves to remind me about whenever he gets the chance.

"I'm serious," he says now, setting the plate of mozzarella sticks in the window before turning and grabbing the next order slip out of the Micros printer. "Entropy, beating back chaos in the universe, all of that. I liked hearing about it."

That stops me. "Yeah?" I ask, a little bit flattered in spite of myself.

"Yeah," Miles echoes. Then, flicking an exaggerated gaze up and down my body: "All that nerd talk was kind of hot."

And there he is: the real Miles. "Okay, then!" I say, pulling off my plastic gloves and tossing them into the trash can. "Enough, thank you. I'm going to go do my actual job now. Try not to light yourself on fire back here. You think you can manage that?"

Miles laughs, the deep rumble as always a little surprising—how grown-up it sounds, maybe, compared to the rest of him. "You know you love me, Rachel Walls."

"I don't, in fact!" I head through the swinging door into the dining room before he can answer, ignoring the arch, knowing look Nonna shoots me from her station behind the counter—the same look she gives me every time she overhears me talking to Miles.

And just like always, I pretend to retch.

To be fair, it's not like Miles is objectively disgusting or anything—in fact, he's got something of a fan club at DiPasquale's, this group of sophomore girls who post up at the corner booth on the nights he's working, drinking pop after pop and craning their necks for a glimpse at him through the service window. He's just so completely *obnoxious.* He's one of those guys who loves to play devil's advocate for the sake of recreation. He wears the same *Winter Is Coming* T-shirt every single day. He's smart—he literally built a whole computer in his basement last year—but he barely graduated because he couldn't be bothered to do his work.

He's also literally the only boy to ever pay any kind of attention to me in my entire life, but that's neither here nor there.

Nonna ignores my Oscar-worthy mime skills and turns back to her conversation—she's gabbing with one of our seasonal regulars, an older guy who spends a few early summer weeks here every year. He says something and Nonna leans in and giggles, her shiny gray hair swinging as she tilts her head to the side.

Giggles.

"Am I getting a new grandpa?" I tease her once the guy is seated across the crowded dining room. "Seriously, what was that?"

"Listen to you, Judge Judy," Nonna says, swatting me on the butt with a laminated menu. "It was flirting. And you should try it sometime."

"Why would I do that, exactly?" Who would I do it with, is more like it.

"It's fun," Nonna says simply. "And sometimes it's good to know you've still got it."

I'm about to reply when I'm cut off by a spray of raucous laughter. I glance across the restaurant, my heart falling all at once directly out of my butt. Clayton Carville is parked in an overflowing booth beside the window, Bethany squished in beside him and Spencer Thomas on her other side. The laughter was hers, blond head thrown back and one hand reaching out playfully to swat at Clayton's cheek.

So. I guess they didn't fight after all.

"Why don't you head out?" Nonna asks quietly. She leans forward against the counter, nudging my shoulder with her own. "Mia will be here in twenty minutes to help me. Go be with your friends." She glances toward the front booth.

I shake my head, my cheeks burning. "We both know they aren't my friends."

Nonna shrugs. "Things can change."

I purse my lips but say nothing. It sounds ridiculous to say I didn't have time for friends in high school. I made space for Ruoxi, didn't I? Same as she made space for me. Still, more often than not, the idea of trying to widen my social circle seemed like a giant waste of energy. Why would I spend a perfectly good study hall period trying to make stilted conversation with someone who probably didn't even want to talk to me when there were AP tests to take, essays to write, college admissions committees to impress? Why go through the trouble of putting myself out there—why risk the rejection, and the embarrassment, and the hurt—when I could already imagine exactly what it was going to be like? After all, I knew my classmates. I'd scrolled their Instagram feeds, heard them chat to one another in the bathroom at school, watched them fight and make up from the hidden comfort of my bedroom window. If I didn't think about it too much, it was almost the same thing as experiencing them myself.

"Well," Nonna says now, "if you're going to stay, make a round, will you, Patatina?" She slides the Italian soda pitcher across the counter in my direction. "I'd do it myself, but my knees are giving me grief."

She's lying and we both know it—she ran three miles this morning, same as she has every day of her life—but she's got it in her head that if I make the rounds and pour their soda, Bethany and her friends will miraculously become my bosom buddies, triggering a movie montage soundtracked to Sara Bareilles where we give each other makeovers and have pillow fights and reunite in ten years to hold each other's babies.

Still, a thing about Nonna is that it's generally less complicated to just do the thing she asks, so I grab the pitcher without complaint. I haven't made it three steps when Bethany perks up like a prairie dog. "Excuse me?" she calls, waving one manicured hand in my direction. "Could we get some more of that?"

I turn toward their booth and see that Clayton is looking at me. He lifts his chin in recognition, though I'm not sure if the expression on his achingly symmetrical face is more *Hey, girl whose graduation speech I enjoyed yesterday* or *Hey, creepy stalker lady, please don't kidnap me and lock me in your basement.* Honestly, it could be either one.

Pull it together, Walls. "Sure thing," I mutter, hefting the pitcher a bit higher and heading over. My heart is beating too fast and my face is too warm. I reach toward the first glass I see, which is Bethany's, but the angle is weird with the booth so crowded and my arm tenses and shakes. *Be careful not to—*

The pitcher tips and, before I can right it, spills.

An entire pitcher of ice and soda.

Onto Clayton.

Carville's.

Lap.

Bethany shoves Spencer out of the way before leaping from the table with a shrill, piercing squeal. Shock gives way to anger as her gaze settles on me. Meanwhile, the others—Tricia Whitman, I register dimly, and Trevor Cheng—react just as quickly, scrambling up with a series of expletives and shouts.

Clayton's face twists and contorts, his green eyes widening. But he can't stand up because he's too far into the booth next to the wall.

"Oh shit! I am so sorry." I turn and grab a stack of napkins off a neighboring table, not bothering to ask permission from the people sitting there. "That was totally my fault. I just . . ." I come at him with the napkins, trying to help soak up the worst of the damage.

His eyes widen further.

A beat too late—*way, way too late*—I realize I'm now clutching a fistful of soggy napkins in the *very near* vicinity of Clayton Carville's junk.

"Oh my God." This cannot be happening. It just . . . I refuse. "I'm . . ." I pull my hand away like it's on fire, except it's actually the rest of my body that's burning. "I was trying to . . . I . . ."

The usual hum of voices, the jostling of ice cubes in glasses, the scrape of knives against plates, all of it has stopped. It's a silence that's only broken by the sloppy thud of soggy napkins when they fall from my hand. "I'm just going to . . ." I gesture vaguely in the direction of the kitchen. "Yeah. Okay."

I don't bother waiting to watch his expression change—I don't think his eyes could get any bigger now, lest they fall out of his head entirely and go rolling across the linoleum—before I turn around and book it toward the relative safety of the bussing station. Never have I been so grateful for that cheap polyester tablecloth hanging from its three-dollar tension rod. The smell of stale garlic and olive oil is permanently infused into the fabric, but for the moment, it offers a spot to disappear.

I lean on the narrow counter next to a tub of dirty dishes, digging the heels of my hands into my eyeballs. I can probably hide out back here until Clayton and his friends leave, right? They can't possibly stick around that much longer. I dig my phone out of my back pocket and text Ruoxi about what happened, but I can tell by the way there's no delivery confirmation that she's got her phone turned off already.

And just like that, I am officially out of friends.

Finally I hear Bethany's voice up at the register.

"We'll, ah, comp you those sodas," Nonna assures her.

Then I hear the jangle of the bells over the door as they all head out into the parking lot. I let out a long, shaky breath, scrubbing my soda-sticky hands through my hair before finally pulling back the curtain—

And nearly crash right into Clayton, who's just coming out of the bathroom with an enormous wet stain covering his entire crotch.

"I'm sorry," I say immediately, holding both hands up to show I'm unarmed. "Really. For spilling on you and for"—*What, Rachel? Nearly jumping to third base in your place of business with a stack of Sysco two-ply napkins?*—"all of it."

"It's fine," Clayton says with a shake of his head. "Really, don't worry about it."

"Oh, I'll worry about it," I assure him. "Like . . . for the rest of my life, probably. I'll be moldering away in the nursing home, and I won't know my own name or how to feed myself, but I will remember this."

Clayton laughs, though I'm not actually joking. "Honestly," he says, "I've had an entire cooler of Gatorade dumped on me at games before. This was nothing."

"Well." I duck my head, wiping my palms on my cheap black work pants. God, why does he have to be so gracious? Why can't he just be a dick so I can move on with my life? "Thank you."

I'm expecting him to go, but instead he looks around the restaurant for a moment, taking in the dessert case full of tiramisu and cannoli, and the black-and-white photos of Venice, and the community bulletin board in the foyer with its flyer for dog walkers and a local kids theater production of *Fiddler on the Roof.* "So you work here, huh?" he asks.

"Yup," I say, leaving out the part where this isn't actually the first time I've been his waitress. He came in with his parents and sister one Sunday night halfway through junior year, all of them sitting at a four-top near the TV and ordering a plain pie and Caesar salads. They fought, I remember suddenly, his mom and dad hissing at each other in low voices I couldn't totally make out no matter how long I lingered, wiping and rewiping nearby tables. Somehow I'd totally forgotten that until right this minute, like it never properly synthesized with all the other information I carry around about Clayton inside my head. "My parents own it."

Clayton nods. "That's cool."

"It has its moments," I agree. "I mean, today I dropped a full pitcher of Italian soda on a guy from my high school, so . . ."

He laughs again then, his voice gravelly and the tiniest bit hoarse; that's two genuine laughs out of Clayton Carville in one conversation, for those of you playing along at home. I'm feeling pretty freaking pleased with myself until he opens his mouth again. "You know," he says, and his tone is so, so easy, "next time, you should think about coming to the party instead of watching it from across the creek."

Oh, just kill me. I open my mouth to deny it even as I'm flushing red and blotchy all over, but what the hell am I going to say? He *saw* me. "Busted," I admit, covering my face with one hand. "I'm sorry. God, you must think I am such a basket case."

"Nah." Clayton shakes his head. "That's not what I think." Then, before I can even begin to try and figure out what *that* means: "Hey," he says, "you know my buddy Spence? The guy who was just here with me?"

"The one who's probably waiting for you outside right now?" *Wondering why you're wasting time talking to Westfield's most awkward recent graduate?*

"Yeah, him." Clayton smiles. "He's actually having some people over tonight, if you want to stop by."

My eyebrows almost evacuate my face entirely; I can literally feel them packing their bags and hitting the road. "You're inviting me to a party?" I can't help but ask.

Clayton tilts his head to the side, looking at me a little oddly. "I mean, why not?" he asks, like it's just that simple. "Is that okay?"

"Yeah, no, it's fine, I just—" I break off, imagining it in spite of myself: the crush of people and the sour reek of beer, the noisy assault on my nervous system.

The weight of Clayton's arm slung around my shoulders. The press of that soft, plush-looking mouth against mine.

I'm about to tell him maybe—holy crap, am I really about to tell him maybe?—when the glass door to the restaurant opens, the chimes above it breaking a spell like a hypnotist pulling a volunteer from a trance. "Clay," Bethany calls—her tone impatient as she leans in through the doorway, slinky as a wildcat in a white T-shirt that makes her peachy skin look impossibly tan. "You coming or what?" Her gaze flicks to me, back to Clayton. "Everything okay?"

"We're good," Clayton promises. "I'll be right there."

Bethany eyes us for another minute, unconvinced. "Okay, but hurry up," is all she says.

Once she's gone again, I shake my head, good sense flooding back in all at once like a dam breaking. What exactly was I about to get myself into?

"I have to work tonight," I lie, shrugging and crinkling my nose like I'm disappointed—and I am, a little bit, though I don't know if I could explain exactly why. "Thanks for the invite, though."

"Yeah, no problem," Clayton says, like it's no skin off his back either way—and it isn't, most likely. He probably walks around inviting people to parties everywhere he goes. He probably invited his *mailman*. It doesn't mean anything. "He lives on Lilac Court, if you change your mind."

"I know," I blurt out, then shake my head. God, could I be more of a weirdo? "I mean—"

"It's cool, Rach," Clayton says, shaking his head and smiling again, saving me from myself. "Have a good night."

"You too," I manage—at least, I think I do; I'm too distracted by that *Rach* to know for sure. I stand in the doorway of the restaurant for a long time after Clayton heads out into the parking lot, watching the summer breeze rustle the leafy green trees on the other side of the glass.

※

Here is what I know: Clayton is, at the very least, still hanging out with Bethany. There's a very real possibility that they're together. But also, Clayton definitely invited me to Spencer Thomas's party. Right?

My plan was to spend tonight Netflix and chilling—there's a documentary about rescue workers in Syria that's been on my radar forever—but even propped up in bed with a to-go container of leftover garlic knots, I can't relax. My bedroom feels overstuffed all of a sudden, the various flotsam of my life closing in and making me claustrophobic: the first-place science fair ribbon pinned to the corkboard. The National Honor Society T-shirt slung over the chair. Evidence of everything I've done—and everything I haven't—surrounding me on all four sides.

All at once, I climb out of bed and start pulling every piece of clothing I own from the closet, sorting it all into two giant keep-or-toss piles on the carpet. I do school papers next, then makeup. I've just started on books when Mom taps two fingers against my doorframe, an expression on her face that suggests she's been watching me for a while. "I hope you're thanking everything for its service," she teases, coming into the room and surveying the damage.

"Obviously," I say with a smile. "I'm also folding my socks into origami swans."

"You can do mine next, how about." She checks her watch. "Thrift store should be open for another couple of hours," she reports. "Want to go do a drop, maybe get some ice cream at Moxie's on the way back?"

"I'll have to check my very busy calendar," I say. "Oh look. It's wide open."

Mom smiles, but there's this weird sadness behind it that I can't tell if I'm imagining or not. I guess I can't really blame her: After all, her seventeen-year-old daughter is spending her first Saturday night after high school graduation Marie Kondo-ing her bedroom. "Let me know when you're ready to go," is all she says.

I was invited to a party tonight! I almost call down the hallway behind her. *By Clayton Carville!*

I just . . . decided not to go.

I turn back to my overstuffed bookshelves, keeping Emma Straub and Alice Walker and tossing a Jonathan Franzen that my ill-advised AP LitComp teacher tried to convince me I might enjoy, before reaching a yellowing paperback I don't immediately recognize: *A Season of Yes!* by Dr. Paula Prescott. The cover shows a woman with feathered hair, blue eye shadow, and a pair of oversized turquoise glasses that scream 1982, blithely resting her chin on her hand.

I pick it up, turning it over to peer at the back copy. Who in their right mind would ever take advice from this woman?

Still, flipping through the first few pages, I see that entire paragraphs have been underlined and the margins are filled up with notes. "Trust the freedom!" is there in Nonna's tight penmanship. Well, there's my answer, I guess. I'm about to chuck it aside into the return-to-the-living-room pile when an underlined passage catches my eye: *The freedom to say "Yes!" to your own life is also the freedom to embrace your true self. If you're feeling stuck, if you're feeling stagnant, if you're feeling like your potential is being wasted, then this book is for you.*

Dr. Paula outlines a three-step plan for success with her process, but essentially it seems to boil down to this: We are, as Aristotle said, what we repeatedly do. Therefore, if we repeatedly say yes to opportunities, people, and experiences, we will become our truest, fullest selves.

I think about that for a moment, sitting down on the edge of the mattress. About the last four years, and the thirteen that came before them. Sure, the process I adopted for myself of saying no to basically everything earned me the title of valedictorian and admission to my dream school. But it also got me . . . here.

Alone.

I fan through the pages with one thumb—breathing in the old-book smell of them, debating. What if Dr. Paula is right?

What if just once I said . . . yes?

I dig my phone out of my pocket and frown at the clock on the screen. It's only seven now. I could go with my mom to the thrift store, get a scoop of double chocolate from Moxie's, and settle in with my Syria documentary.

Or I could take Clayton up on his invitation.

Before I can talk myself out of it, I'm tugging a fleece over my head and smudging on some makeup, digging a flavored ChapStick I tossed twenty minutes ago out of the garbage and slicking it over my lips. I pause in front of the mirror in the hallway, twisting my reddish hair around my fingertips in the hopes of it looking more "effortlessly curly" and less "before picture in a Frizz Ease ad."

"Not getting any better than this," I mutter, and thump down the stairs into the living room.

My parents are sitting on the sofa watching a *CSI* rerun on cable, which is frankly exactly the kind of programming I might have joined them for on a normal evening. Nonna is parked in her easy chair, working a cross-stich that reads *Smash the Patriarchy* in precise, scrolling script. "You ready?" my mom asks, sliding her feet out of the slippers she's wearing with her jeans and button-down and glancing around for her sneakers.

I shake my head. "Can we rain-check for tomorrow?" I ask, suddenly embarrassed. "Turns out I actually . . . have plans."

"Of course." She tilts her head to the side, curious. Nonna has looked up, interest written all over her face. "You going somewhere?"

"Some people are hanging out," I explain, trying to sound casual. "I thought I might stop by."

Mom stares at me for a long moment, like I just told her I was going to go hang gliding or model for a photoshoot involving bikinis and muscle cars. "Okay," she says finally, remembering herself. "That sounds great. You need a ride somewhere?"

I shake my head. "I can walk."

"Your phone is charged?"

"Yup," I promise.

"And you'll call us if anything—"

"Mom!" I laugh a little. "I'm on the fence about this anyway, okay? Don't make me rethink it any more than I already am."

"Go!" Nonna hollers, waving her cross-stitch at me like a flag at a drag race. "Be young. Have fun."

I wave goodbye, bounding out the door and down the front steps before I can talk myself out of it. I don't have to look back to know both she and my mom are watching me from the front window. I try to ignore them, and the butterflies in my stomach, as I head down the street in the pink summer twilight—toward my first high school party, and whatever might be waiting for me there.

4

$\mathcal{I}$'m a little more than two blocks away from Spencer Thomas's house when the doubt in my head gets loud enough to drown out even the cheeriest of Paula Prescott's frothy affirmations. Holy crap, what am I *doing*? Am I really just about to stroll into this stranger's house—completely solo—like I'm a person who belongs there in any capacity whatsoever? I might as well walk into freaking Mordor. I should just turn back now. If I hurry, I can still catch the end of *CSI*.

But then I remember: Clayton invited me. And I'm a yes person now.

I'm just rounding the corner onto Lilac Court when someone calls out behind me: "Yo, Jacobs!" I turn around to see Ethan Watson, another soccer player, trailing me onto the cul-de-sac. "Oh," he says, cocking his head when he realizes it's me instead. "Sorry.

Thought you were someone else." His gaze flicks to Spencer's house, then back at me. "You going to Spence's?"

This is it. No turning back.

"Um . . . yes?" I try.

I'm fully expecting a weird look or even a flat-out *"Why?"* but Ethan only nods. "Sweet," he says, falling into step beside me. He's wearing khaki shorts and a University of Michigan hoodie, an immaculate pair of sneakers glowing almost blindingly white against his dark brown skin. "Hey, good job yesterday."

"Thanks," I say, surprised.

"I would have fully shat my pants if I had to get up and talk in front of all those people." He opens the front door of Spencer's house with easy authority, ushering me grandly inside. "After you."

I've actually been to Spencer's house once before, to work on a group project sophomore year—a health class presentation on the dangers of smoking for which I put together a fifteen-minute PowerPoint that was, in retrospect, possibly a little overwrought. "You don't think this is . . . a lot?" I remember Spencer asking, squinting at my laptop screen as Sarah McLachlan's "Angel" played mournfully over pictures of calcified lungs and regretful-looking emphysemics. But you know what? I got us all an A.

In any case, the house is somehow even bigger than I remember it: new construction with a massive foyer and tons of windows, the rooms all flowing graciously into one another instead of crowding in at weird angles, like they do at my house. I stand awkwardly at the foot of the curving staircase for a moment, my eyes raking over the huge abstract paintings and the space-age chandelier. Ethan's halfway into the dining room before he realizes I'm not behind him. "Yo," he says again, pulling a six-pack of Bud Light out of his backpack. "You coming or what?"

I blink. "Yes!" I repeat—it comes out easier this time—and follow him toward the back of the house.

Ethan leads me through the kitchen, which is straight out of a home renovation show, and down a carpeted staircase into the giant basement. I came here fully anticipating a rager, a hundred strangers doing kegstands and throwing up into potted plants like something out of the opening montage of a '90s teen movie, but I'm surprised to find only about a dozen people scattered throughout the cavernous space, which boasts at least two bedrooms plus a living area with a leather sectional the size of an aircraft carrier and an entire second kitchen. Tricia Whitman and a couple of her friends cluster around the pool table, where Spencer and Trevor Cheng are arguing mildly over which one of them is cheating. Sierra Woodfolk and Joanna Green are making pizza rolls under the broiler while a couple of soccer bros play *Warcraft* on the big-screen TV.

In theory, the whole scene should ease my raging anxiety— after all, isn't a chill, mellow hangout easier to navigate than the alternative?—but instead I just feel like I'm sticking out way more than I would have at Bethany's last night. These people are all *friends* with each other. And I'm . . .

What, exactly?

I glance around for Clayton—I've been glancing around for

Clayton since the second I walked through the door—but I don't see him. I'm wondering if maybe I should look upstairs, if maybe there's another group of people around here somewhere, when James Chemaly ambles over in basketball shorts and a T-shirt, red plastic cup in one hand. "Yo, E!" he says to Ethan, his vowels just a little bit loose. He looks at me, squinting a little. "And . . . other girl."

"Rachel," I introduce myself, even though we've definitely had at least three classes together over the course of our high school careers. He used to date Miriam Harris, but she's a year older than us, and judging from the way she stopped showing up on his Snapchat around Christmas, I'm pretty sure they broke up when she went to college.

James nods. "Cool," he says blandly, then turns around to fix himself another drink.

Oookay, then. I look back at Ethan, hoping for reinforcement, but he's wandered across the basement to sit with the *Warcraft* guys, leaving me standing alone beside a mostly empty bag of Tostitos. I help myself to a couple of salty shards for lack of anything better to do, praying nobody notices me lurking alone like a giant loser and desperate for someone to talk to in equal amounts. Tricia Whitman lets out a cackle over by the pool table, loud and raucous—and oh God, is she laughing at *me*?

These are not my people. And I do not belong here, not even a little bit. Remind me again why on earth I put myself through this?

That's when I spy Clayton through the open door of one of the bedrooms down the hall.

He's sitting with one knee up on the wrought-iron daybed, his fingers laced with Bethany's, their heads tipped close together as they talk. He's changed his clothes since this afternoon—he would have had to, I think bitterly, since some klutz spilled Italian soda all over the ones he was wearing—his gray Henley pushed to the elbows and an embroidery floss friendship bracelet looped around one tawny wrist. He's looking at her as if she's the only other person in the entire state of Michigan.

He's looking at her as if she's the only other person in the world.

Bethany shakes her head, raises her narrow shoulders like she's pleading. "I don't know what to *do*" is all I hear her say. I wonder if they're fighting again, not that it matters.

Not that any of this has anything to do with me at all.

Clayton's about to respond when Spencer raises his voice over by the pool table: "Dude, you're full of shit!" he tells Trevor, neither of them playing around anymore. Bethany throws her hands up in exasperation at the noise—getting up and kicking the bedroom door closed, locking herself and Clayton away from the rest of the party.

But in the second before it shuts, Clayton looks down the hallway—

And sees me.

Oh God. My stomach turns, the garlic knots I ate earlier threatening to repeat themselves all over Spencer's parents' tasteful Berber carpet. The idea of Clayton knowing I'm here—that I actually *came,* like his invitation was real and not the conversational equivalent of asking a grocery store cashier how her day is—is unbearable. It feels like my bones are made of sawdust. It feels like my skin is too tight. Who was I kidding? I am not a yes person. I am a no person. I have always been a no person. I will always be a no person.

I take a deep breath—trying to focus on the task in front of me, same as I have in the face of every difficult exam or high-pressure presentation in the last four years. I can get out of here. All I have to do is backtrack across the basement as quickly as possible, find my way to the front door, and spend the rest of the summer pretending none of this ever happened. I'm nearly to the stairs when—

"Rachel?"

I turn around to see Carrie Whiting-Bryant sitting on the sectional with her bare feet up on the coffee table, holding a koozie-wrapped beer can in one brown hand. Carrie Whiting-Bryant, who used to be one of my very best friends. "What are you doing here?" she asks, surprised but not unfriendly. She stands up, wobbling once before righting herself and crossing the basement in my direction.

"Oh . . . I . . . um . . ." I shake my head and press my lips together. I don't know why the sight of her face of all things is what makes me feel like I might be about to burst into tears. "You know, I was just wondering the same thing."

"Fair enough." Carrie looks at me, frowning a little—actually *seeing* me, I think, more than anyone has since I walked through the door. "You okay?"

"Walls!" Ethan calls out before I can figure out how to answer, plucking darts from a dartboard on the other side of the room. "You're still here." He lines up and takes his shot, hitting the skinny part of a black rectangle. "I thought maybe you'd split already."

"Wait," Carrie says, her long braids swinging as she looks back and forth between us. "You two came together?"

"What?" Ethan and I answer in unison. "No."

"Just walked in at the same time," he explains, then points to the dartboard. "So, ladies. Three-oh-one. Who's playing?"

I shake my head. "Not me," I say firmly, glancing again toward the staircase. Once they're distracted, nobody will notice me slipping out. "You guys have fun, though."

"Oh, come on," Ethan says, holding three darts out in my direction. "This game's got your name written all over it. It's all math."

"Math, and making sure nobody is standing between you and the dartboard," Carrie puts in. She smirks at Ethan. "Remember when Spence got one stuck in his—"

"Nobody wants to remember that!" Spencer yells from across the room.

"Walls," Ethan says again, still holding the darts out like an offering. "Are you really going to leave a man hanging here?"

I glance from the dartboard to Carrie, who's arching her perfectly groomed eyebrows in invitation. On one hand, all I want is to slink home and lick my wounds in the comfort of my freshly decluttered bedroom.

On the other: What would Dr. Paula do?

"Okay," I hear myself say. "How does it work, exactly?"

We play for the next half hour or so, Carrie acting as referee and cheerleader. By the time Ethan heads off to find himself another drink, the worst of my horror and embarrassment has leached away. Still, I can't help but steal a glance in the direction of the bedroom Bethany and Clayton are in. The door is still resolutely closed.

"So," Carrie says once it's just the two of us, hopping up onto a barstool in one sleek movement like a cat climbing onto a window-sill, taking a delicate sip of her beer. "What's new?"

I hesitate, caught up weirdly short by the question. It feels like everything I might tell her is both too big and too small to mention, after all this time. "Not much, I guess."

Carrie snorts. "Seriously?"

"What?" I feel my spine straighten.

"I mean, nothing," she says, shrugging elegantly inside her silky black tank top. She was a ballet dancer back in middle school, but all her social media accounts are set to private so I'm not actually sure if she still does it or not. Something about the way she moves her body makes me think the answer is yes. "I mean, it's literally been three and a half years since we had a conversation, but if 'not much' is the answer you want to go with, you do you I guess."

I huff a breath out, weirdly offended. *I haven't actually changed that much since then,* I want to tell her. *I think maybe that's part of the problem.*

"I mean, I got my period finally," I inform her imperiously. "If that's the kind of update you're after."

That makes her laugh—the kind of belly laugh that used to get us in trouble at sleepovers, one of her dads perpetually yelling up the stairs for us to pipe down and go to sleep. "Weirdo," she says, but her tone makes it sound like an endearment, the kind of thing you'd say to someone you love. "I'm glad for you. Welcome to womanhood, et cetera."

I snort. "Thank you."

Carrie takes one last pull from her can and tugs it out of its koozie, hopping off her stool and holding the empty up in my direction. "I'm going to grab another," she announces.

"Oh," I say, trying to hide my disappointment. I have missed her, I realize suddenly. Maybe more than I ever let myself think about. "Okay."

Carrie rolls her eyes, gesturing widely in the direction of the kitchen. "Do you want to come?"

"Me?" My head snaps back in her direction.

"No, the other lost-looking white girl at this party," Carrie deadpans. "Yes, Rach. You."

I smile sheepishly and follow her across the basement, watching as the *Warcraft* bros scoot out of her way without her even having to ask. She fishes two cans of Coors out of the fridge before digging another koozie out of a kitchen drawer and handing it over. It's startling to me how comfortable they all seem to be here: draped over the sectional, sprawled out on the rug. The only person whose kitchen drawers I ever would have dug through were . . .

Well. Carrie's.

She helps herself to a bag of Fritos before leading me through the sliding glass doors and out onto the patio, where a giant inground pool shimmers in the moonlight, the smell of warm grass and chlorine thick in the summer air. She sits down on a lounge chair, nodding with her chin at the one beside her as she cracks her beer and takes a sip.

"So you didn't actually answer me," she says once she's swallowed, holding the bag of Fritos out in my direction. "About what you're doing here, I mean. Not that I'm not glad you came—trust me, I get tired of seeing the same ugly faces every single weekend—but still."

I shrug, running my thumb around the edge of my beer can instead of actually opening it. "Just . . . thought I'd try something new, I guess."

"You hate new things, though." Then she frowns and shakes her head, looking annoyed at herself. "Sorry. That was bitchy. Obviously people can change. You're allowed to have changed."

I smile. "That's the thing, though: I haven't really. I just . . . started thinking that maybe I'd like to? I don't know. Anyway, Clayton invited me—"

Carrie looks at me sideways. "Clayton did?"

"Um, yeah," I say, immediately regretting saying anything. Carrie and Bethany have been best friends since sophomore year. Already I'm imagining Carrie reporting this conversation back to her, the two of them doubled over laughing at how delusional I am. "I don't actually think it was a real invitation, though. I think he kind of did it by accident."

Carrie wrinkles her nose. "I doubt it," she says, digging a handful of Fritos out of the bag. "Clay isn't really the type to do anything by accident. He's like you that way, actually."

Before I can ask what she means, the patio doors slide open— Spencer and James and Trevor all spilling out into the yard, Ethan trailing them with a Bluetooth speaker in one hand. "This where the party is?" James calls, pulling off his T-shirt and sneakers. His back is so skinny I can see each individual knob of his spine.

"You know it," Carrie says with a roll of her eyes. "We came out here specifically hoping you'd follow us and cause a commotion."

James ignores her, cannonballing sloppily into the deep end. "You guys getting in?" he calls once he's surfaced, spitting a long stream of water out like a fountain.

"No thank you," Carrie says as the rest of them follow suit, shucking their shirts—and, in Trevor's case, his shorts, revealing a pair of bright blue boxers printed with cartoon robots. It's the most amount of boy skin I've seen in, well, ever, and I glance away, scratching at the back of my neck and trying not to stare. "Somehow the idea of stewing in a bunch of water that's just been in your mouth is not that appealing to me."

"Your loss, chica." James floats on his back for a moment, his pale chest gleaming in the patio lights. "What about you, Rachel?" he asks, raising his eyebrows in my direction. "You coming?"

"Me?" I blink, surprised. It's funny, I think, that apparently all I needed to remove my invisibility cloak was someone like Carrie sitting next to me. But I don't have a suit with me, first of all, and even if I did . . . "I don't think so."

Carrie and I sit back in our lounge chairs and watch the boys splash around for a moment, an old Harry Styles song echoing out of the tinny speakers into the quiet night. Carrie takes a long sip of her beer, eyes my untouched can. "Tastes better cold, you know."

"That is . . . what I hear."

Carrie snorts. "You really haven't changed, have you," she says, a statement instead of a question. "Menstruation notwithstanding, obviously."

"I mean, I also learned to drive a car." I slip my sandals off and tuck my bare feet underneath me, not wanting to talk about myself anymore. "Not that I *have* one to drive, but. Theoretically." Tricia and her friends have made their way out onto the patio by now, the whole party splashing around in the pool—that is, except Clayton and Bethany, who still haven't made an appearance. I can't help but wonder what exactly they're doing in there, on the daybed alone where nobody can see. "So what are you up to this summer?" I ask.

Carrie shakes her head. "Nothing terribly exciting, I'm sorry to report. Answering phones at the gallery, biding my time until August. You?"

I shrug. "Swap paintings for pizzas, and pretty much exactly that."

"Really?" Carrie raises her eyebrows. "You're working at the restaurant? I would have thought you were headed off somewhere to cure cancer or, like, save the whales."

"Oh, you're hilarious." I make a face.

Carrie grins. "At the very least I'm sure you've got work to do on your Fulbright application—"

"Rude!" I chide, throwing a Frito in her direction, though the truth is it's nice to be teased by her. Ruoxi is wonderful, but she's also completely, unrelentingly earnest. I forgot what it felt like to get ribbed by a friend. "Where are you going in the fall?"

"Art Institute of Chicago," she tells me. "I got waitlisted, but they emailed two days ago to say I'm in."

"Carrie, that's great!" I pick my still-full beer can up off the concrete, clink it with hers. "Is that what you want to do?" I ask as Trevor executes a particularly painful-sounding belly flop and everyone groans. "Run a gallery like your dads?"

She shrugs, drawing one long leg up and resting her chin on her knee. "I have no idea, honestly."

"Doesn't that scare you?"

"I think it would scare me more to have my whole life plotted out, honestly," she says. "What about you? Still headed for law school?"

"That is the plan," I tell her.

"Mergers and acquisitions, or whatever?"

I shake my head. "Criminal defense, I think. Maybe death penalty stuff? Or something around mass incarceration, I'm not sure."

"Seriously?" Carrie's eyebrows flicker, like possibly I've surprised her for the first time all night. "That's kind of cool."

She's starting to say something else when Ethan smacks his wet hands on the pool deck. "Hey!" he yells over to us. "Enough girl talk! Everybody into the pool!"

I shake my head again, but Carrie heaves a loud, theatrical sigh, unfolding her long limbs and getting to her feet before reaching for the button on her denim shorts. "All right, all right," she tells Ethan. "Don't get your panties in a twist." Then, looking at me: "What do you say?"

"Wait, seriously?" I startle, shaking my head on instinct. "What happened to like, not wanting to be contaminated by James's germs?"

"I'm over it," Carrie says with a shrug. She shimmies out of her shorts and peels her tank top over her head, revealing a practical-looking black sports bra. "You coming?"

"I'm not getting naked in front of all these people!" I hiss.

"Then wear your clothes in, Princess." She holds her hand out, an invitation. "Come on," she presses. "You're trying new things this summer, right?"

"I mean, sure, but—"

"So prove it."

I hesitate for a moment, torn between every instinct in my body and the thought of Dr. Paula Prescott sitting on a lounge chair in her power suit, urging me to open myself to new experiences. Just say yes, right? Finally I scrunch my nose and stand up, tugging my fleece over my head. "All right. Let's do this."

"There you go!" Carrie says.

"Yeah, Walls!" Ethan yells, drunkenly delighted with himself. Trevor lets out a hoot. Tricia and her friends are eyeing me warily from the hot tub, but when I catch her gaze and smile sheepishly, I'm surprised to see her smiling back.

"On three, okay?" Carrie instructs, dragging me over to the edge of the deep end. "One . . . two . . ." And then she tugs my arm and we're falling in together, the shock of the chilly water and the thrill of jumping in at all. My scalp tingles, goose bumps springing up all over my body. My jeans weigh about a thousand pounds.

"You didn't say three!" I sputter as I surface, but I'm laughing. Carrie only grins.

❋

The house is mostly dark by the time I get home, the porch light winking above the front door as I slip my squelching shoes off. Upstairs I change into dry pajamas and scoop my damp hair into a knot, glancing at the book still sitting on top of my bed. "All right," I tell Dr. Paula grudgingly. "You win this round, I'll grant you that." Things definitely didn't go quite as I'd hoped tonight— the bedroom door was open when we all finally traipsed back into the basement, Clayton and Bethany nowhere to be found—but on the whole, it wasn't actually a disaster.

I'm just climbing under the covers when my phone buzzes with a text from Carrie: **Glad you came tonight** , it says.

I chew my thumbnail for a moment, dumbly pleased in spite of myself. We exchanged numbers before, but I never expected her to actually text me. Obviously I don't think this means our friendship is back on, or whatever. But it's nice to know we can go off to college without some weird, unfinished fug hanging between us.

Yeah, I type finally. **I'm glad I did too.**

I turn out the light and burrow under the covers. I sleep better than I have in a long time.

5

"So how was the party?" Miles asks the following morning. He's washing dishes in the kitchen at the restaurant, loading the rack with a dozen pebbled plastic cups, and his voice is the singsong tease of a person who thinks he knows something. "Was the discussion of grain alcohol chasers absolutely *scintillating*?"

I blink, a half-assembled ham-and-cheese Gondola clutched in one hand. "How did you even know I was *at* a party last night?"

"I have my sources," he says cryptically. Then he shrugs and holds up his phone, the screen of which is completely shattered—an unfortunate mosh pit incident, claims Miles, though I blatantly saw it fall out of his pocket in the parking lot one day last spring. "You were basically all over the internet."

"Wait, really?" I grab the phone and scroll through his feed—where, sure enough, there's a somewhat blurry Boomerang of Carrie and me jumping into Spencer's pool. "Oh," I say. "Well. Yeah."

"Whose house is that, Spencer Thomas's?" Miles strokes an imaginary beard. "Not your usual crowd."

His tone is totally mild, but still something about the way he says it irks me—how sure he seems, maybe, how certain he knows exactly who I am and what I'm capable of. "And who would my usual crowd be, exactly?"

"I mean, nobody," Miles deadpans immediately. "That's what I'm saying."

I huff a breath, stung. On one hand, it's just Miles. I don't care what he thinks of me. Still, it's not like I'm crazy about the ideas of having no friends or suitors being my defining characteristic. "You know what, Miles," I snap, "I don't actually remember asking you for your opinion. And I don't actually see how it's any of your business what I do."

I'm expecting an argument, but Miles holds up two soapy hands. "Sorry, sorry," he says, conceding the point so easily that for a moment I almost feel bad about sniping at him. "I'm happy for you, if you had fun." Then his lips twist. "Next time you should consider taking more of your clothes off, though. You know. For the cameras."

"Ugh." I shove the half-constructed Gondola in his direction. "You're foul."

"And you're extremely easy to rile up," he says, drying his hands.

"I'm serious," I say, emphatically uncharmed. I'll be honest— sometimes I find it kind of fun, whatever weird back-and-forth thing Miles and I have going on. At the very least, it helps pass the time during lulls at the restaurant. But then other times it's like he's totally committed to being the grossest, most annoying version of himself, like he's actively trying to put me off. "Why do you always have to do that?"

"Do what?" he asks, plastering an innocent face on.

"That," I say, waving my hand vaguely.

Miles sets the Gondola down on the counter in its paper tray, a beat passing like he's actually thinking about it. "Deflect?"

"I mean, I was going to say *be yourself*," I fire back, surprised by his vocabulary. "But sure, *deflect* works too."

He shrugs. "Generalized anxiety and oppositional defiant disorder, I guess," he tells me. "At least, that's what my therapist says."

That is . . . not what I was expecting him to say. "Wait," I say again. Since when does Miles go to *therapy*? "Seriously?"

Miles tilts his head to the side, pressing his lips together for a moment before nudging me gently out of the way so he can finish making the sandwich. "Seriously," he says.

"Since when?"

He shrugs, reaching for a handful of shredded lettuce instead of looking at me. "A few months, I guess? After the whole *almost not graduating* thing, it was kind of a condition for my mom not kicking me out of the house."

I gnaw on my thumbnail for a moment, which is definitely a health and safety violation. "Is it because of . . ." I trail off. "Like . . . stuff with your brother?"

Miles smirks down at the counter. "You can say his name, you know. He isn't Voldemort."

"No," I say, embarrassed. "Of course he's not." Tommy is—
was?—three years older than Miles and me. The summer before he
was supposed to leave for Quinnipiac he picked up a rare form of
meningitis from a water bottle at the camp where he was a coun-
selor and spent the last eleven days of his life in a coma at a hospital
on the Upper Peninsula. Miles never talks about him at all.

"Anyway," he says now, his voice bright and booming like a game
show announcer showcasing a brand-new car, "it's actually still un-
clear whether I'm a mess because of *stuff with my brother* or whether
I'm a mess because I'm just, like, a mess. But your hypothesis is
noted for the record." He raises his eyebrows then, mischievous.
"Girls like a messed-up guy, right? Leather jacket, king of pain?"

"You're doing it again," I point out, although the secret truth is
I do actually think he'd look sort of cute in a leather jacket. I bump
his shoulder with mine without quite planning to do it—wanting
him to know I think it's good that he's in therapy. Wanting him to
know I'm sorry about Tommy, even if I never know how to say it
out loud. "Deflecting, I mean."

Miles makes a face, sticking the Italian-flag toothpicks in both
halves of the sandwich and ringing the bell on the counter. "I'm
working on it, okay? I have a little sticker chart and everything."

"Do you really?"

He smiles for real now, his dark eyes catching mine and holding. "No."

We look at each other for another moment, neither one of us

saying anything. I can see his pulse ticking in his neck. It occurs to me that I almost want to tell him about Paula Prescott and my Summer of Yes—to trust him with something, maybe, the way he trusted me with all of this.

"Hey there!" Dad bursts through the back door into the kitchen just then, which is probably for the best. The last thing I need is Miles holding something like that over my head for the rest of the summer, trying to use it as a pretext to convince me we should hold up convenience stores and, like, sleep naked under the stars. "Exactly the two people I was looking for."

"What's up, Mr. Walls?" Miles takes a giant step away from me—shoot, I definitely had not realized how close we were standing—and jams his hands into the pockets of his jeans.

"Come on outside with me for a tick, would ya?" Dad gestures to the back door of the kitchen, where all the deliveries come in. "Your mom can cover the line."

The two of us follow him out the back door and into the service alley, where there's a small truck parked in DiPasquale's designated parking spot. "Are we . . . moving something?" I ask, squinting a bit in the afternoon sun.

"Not exactly," Dad says. "Drum roll, please?"

Miles and I exchange a baffled look. "Uh, what?" I ask.

"Oh, fine." Dad grabs the handle on the moving truck's door and tugs it upward in one swift motion. "Ta-da!"

Inside the otherwise empty cargo hold is a small cart on wheels with a decent-sized chest cooler attached. The whole thing is shiny sea-foam green, with a loopy red DiPasquale's logo painted on the broad side.

"What do you think?" Dad asks, looking openly chuffed with himself.

"Um . . . what is it?" Miles asks, rubbing the back of his neck.

"Well, I've been calling it the Cream Cart," Dad tells him proudly, "but we can change that if you kids can come up with something better." He's almost dancing around the thing, motioning us to step into the truck to check it out. "It's for the summer. A stroke of brilliance if I do say so myself."

He opens the lid to the cooling chest. It's brand-new and divided into two halves: one with four circular holes that look like buckets or vats would fit into them, and the other revealing deep shelved compartments. "The Stracciatella, Gianduja, Fior de Latte, and Pistachio di Bronte go here," Dad explains, pointing to the four round compartments, "and Nonna's lady fingers go on the other side. And voila! A tasty dessert and beach-friendly spin on DiPasquale's signature menu item."

"So . . . ice cream sandwiches?" I ask.

"Ice cream *Gondolas*," Miles corrects, the ghost of a smile playing across his lips. "Gosh, Rachel, get with the program."

"Yes! That's exactly right." Dad is practically doing backflips. "Made with the customer's choice of up to two of our signature gelato flavors and Nonna's delicious cookies. Haven't you noticed her perfecting the recipe?"

I have, actually—I shoved a soggy fistful of them into my mouth last night when I got home from Spencer's party—but I'm still not totally following. "How do we factor into this, exactly?"

Dad explains that this first outing—"The Original Cream Cart," he calls it—is a trial but that he hopes if it's successful enough, next summer he can have two or three of them dotted along the beach-front. "And since the two of you are leaving in the fall and I figured you might not want to spend your last summer cooped up in the restaurant . . ."

"You want us to run it?" I ask.

"Together?" Miles chimes in.

"Exactly," Dad says, pleased that we've finally caught on. "Rachel can be the customer service person and, Miles, you can prepare the orders—since, no offense, your people skills occasionally leave something to be desired."

"He's working on it," I say, glancing at Miles sidelong. He grins at me, quick and gone again, in reply.

"All right," Dad says, clapping his hands like a little kid at—well, at the sight of an ice cream truck. "Let's get this baby ready to go!"

※

Miles and I spend the next hour stocking the cooler and the com-partment where napkins, the Square reader, and extra tools go, making sure the Cream Cart is ready for its maiden voyage to-morrow afternoon. "He must have spent a ton of money on this contraption," I note, eyeing it with no small amount of trepidation. "We're going to have to sell a lot of ice cream sandwiches just to break even."

"Ice cream *Gondolas*," Miles corrects absently, straightening the stack of paper napkins. "Better work on your sales pitch." I wait for him to suggest some perverted thing involving bikinis and whipped cream, but instead he just straightens up, brushing his hands off on the seat of his pants and looking at me. "Hey, can I ask you something?" he says, looking weirdly serious. "Do you have plans ton—"

"Rachel?"

The sound of my name is accompanied by a *knock-knock-knock* on the side of the moving truck. When I poke my head out the back, I'm surprised to see Carrie standing on the concrete in shorts and a T-shirt from last year's Ann Arbor Pride, her braids pulled back with a vintagey-looking scarf. "Hey," she says, waving at Miles before looking back at me. "Sorry, I didn't mean to creep on you. Nonna—I mean, your grandma—said you were out here."

"Oh." I frown, totally flabbergasted by the sight of her. Sure, we talked about maybe hanging out again when we exchanged numbers last night, but honestly I figured it was the same kind of popular-person non-vitation as Clayton asking me to Spencer's party. I definitely wasn't expecting her to actively seek me out not twenty-four hours later. "I mean, hi!" I smile, remembering myself. "Sorry. What's up?"

"A bunch of us are headed to the fair in Douglas," she reports, nodding in the general direction of the parking lot on the side of the building. "I was going to text, but then the restaurant was on the way, so I figured I'd just stop by and see if maybe you wanted to come."

"Oh!" I say again, truly taking advantage of the opportunity to showcase my enviable conversational chops. The Douglas Fair marks the official kickoff to summer in this part of Michigan, though I haven't been since I was probably twelve because it always conflicts with busy season for the restaurant. At least, that's what I told myself. "Like, right now?"

"Yeah, Rachel," Carrie says, with that same tolerant smile from last night—like she thinks I'm a piece of work, maybe, but also like she missed me. "Right now."

I grin back at her; I can't help it. Ruoxi notwithstanding, I can literally count on zero hands how many times I've been invited anywhere over the course of my high school career. And now it's happened twice in as many days.

Still, I find myself glancing at Miles, who's busying himself wiping a scuff off the side of the Cream Cart. It definitely *seemed* like he was about to ask if I wanted to hang out tonight, didn't it? I don't owe him anything, obviously. But it's also possible that, in the split second before Carrie knocked on the side of the truck, I was the tiniest bit intrigued.

"You're more than welcome too, Miles," Carrie says, misinterpreting the look I've shot in his direction, but Miles holds a hand up.

"Can't do carnivals," he says, shaking his head gravely. "Heart condition."

I roll my eyes. "He's deflecting," I report.

"Um, okay." Carrie tilts her head, a little uncertain. "So what do you say?"

This time, I don't even have to wonder what Paula Prescott would want me to do. "Yes," I tell her, hopping out of the truck and down onto the concrete. "Just give me five minutes."

I dig a pair of cutoffs and a wrinkly T-shirt out of my locker, trying with little success to smooth the worst of the creases out before giving up and shaking my hair out of its braid. I kiss Nonna goodbye—"Look at you, Patatina!" she crows, like possibly I'm a toddler learning to use the toilet—and wave to my dad before darting back outside.

"Ready to go?" I ask Carrie, who holds up her car keys in response.

"See ya," Miles calls, still messing around inside the moving truck. I glance back at him one last time before we go.

6

*T*he fair is pretty much exactly the same as I remember it from when I was little: a midway packed with water gun races and win-a-goldfish Ping-Pong ball tosses, the kind of rickety-looking rides that fold out of trucks. The grounds are crowded with locals and a few early season tourists eating corn dogs and funnel cake, the scent of drugstore perfume and cotton candy heavy in the muggy air. A band is set up on a low stage near one end of the field, and Carrie and I stop to listen for a while—two fratty white guys in cowboy hats who advertise themselves as a country ensemble, though their repertoire seems to skew mostly toward Hootie & the Blowfish songs from 1994.

"So who are we waiting for?" I ask finally, scratching a mosquito bite on one calf with the toe of my Converse.

Carrie frowns. "Huh?" she asks distractedly, offering me half of her Sanders hot fudge cream puff.

Welp, I don't need Dr. Paula's book to convince me to say yes to that one. "You said 'a bunch of us' were coming," I remind her, popping it into my mouth and swallowing. "Who's a bunch?"

"Oh." Carrie bites her lip, looking a little bit embarrassed. "All right, I may have overstated. I mean, Ethan and Trevor said maybe they'd stop by, but . . ." She sighs. "I'm kind of talking to this guy and he said he might be here tonight, so I sort of wanted to like, stake the place out." She makes a face. "I know, it's pathetic."

"It's not pathetic," I say immediately. God knows I'm the last person on planet Earth who's in a position to criticize what anyone else does in the name of romantic infatuation. On top of which it's kind of nice, the idea that Carrie trusted me to be her wingwoman. Even if she probably only did it because none of her other friends were around.

"It's . . . whatever." Carrie wipes her hands on the seat of her shorts. "So, hey," she says, nodding at something behind me as the band clangs away at "Only Wanna Be with You" for what I'm pretty sure is the second time in the last twenty minutes, "how do you feel about that?"

I turn around. "The bungee thing?" It's a ride, sort of, this ridiculous reverse-catapult contraption with what looks like a foam hamster ball attached to two giant bungee cords. Two people sit in the ball and then it launches them up and snaps back and forth at a velocity that looks guaranteed to cause traumatic brain injury.

She grins. "It could be fun."

"Yeah," I shoot back, "or it could be awful and we could die."

Carrie cackles. "Nice to see you've held on to your flair for the dramatic after all these years."

"Yeah, well—"

"Carrie!" a guy calls from behind us. "Walls!"

Carrie looks over my shoulder and breaks out into a smile before I can turn to see who's she spotted. Or rather, who spotted us. "What's up?" she calls, lifting her chin in greeting as Ethan ambles over in our direction.

With Clayton trailing directly along behind him.

"Man, Walls," Ethan says before I can properly rearrange my face into anything resembling indifference. "Two days in a row?" He grins. "You stalking me or what?"

"In your dreams maybe," Carrie answers for me. "What's up, Clay?"

"Not much," he says, shaking his head and jamming his hands into his pockets. His gaze flicks in my direction for one achingly brief moment. "Hey, Rachel."

"Hi," I manage. Suddenly all the sadness and disappointment from last night comes rushing back, sucking at my limbs like an undertow. I swallow it down and do my best to put on a smile. He's dating someone, that's all. It's a thing people do.

"So what are you ladies up to?" Ethan asks, taking a sip of his slushie—cherry, judging by the faint red stain on his full lips. He's wearing his Michigan hoodie again, a baseball cap tilted rakishly on his head.

"Just discussing the Ejector, actually," Carrie tells him, tilting her head toward the bungee ride of death. "I'm too scared to do it, but Rachel's freaking obsessed."

"Wait, *what?*" I gape at her for a second, then look back at the guys. "There's no way. She's delusional, truly."

"There's nothing to be embarrassed about," Carrie teases, twisting one of her braids between two fingers. "You're an insatiable thrill seeker, we know."

"Uh-oh," Ethan says, picking up on the bit. "We've got a secret adrenaline junkie on our hands?"

I roll my eyes. "I assure you, that is . . . *emphatically* not the case."

"Aw, I always kind of loved the Ejector," Clayton chimes in, the neon lights studding the ride casting his face in pinks and blues. Up close he's not actually *entirely* symmetrical, I noticed yesterday in the restaurant, with a small constellation of pale freckles clustered just under his right eye. He looks back at me, raises his eyebrows. "You've really never been?"

"Uh, nope," I say, feeling oddly defiant. Probably I've never done a lot of things he's done. "And I never intend to."

"Aw, come on, Walls!" Ethan takes a final noisy slurp of his slushie before dumping the cup into a nearby trash can. "Now you've gotta do it."

"He's right," Carrie says, slinging her fringey suede purse across her body and taking a couple of big steps backward in the direction of the Ejector. "It's time."

I shake my head. "Hard pass."

Carrie is unmoved. "Summer of new experiences!" she crows, and I wince, not exactly dying to let the guys in on my little self-improvement project. "I'm going, you're going, we're all going."

"Carrie—"

"You sure?" Clayton asks—and there's that dimple again, like punctuation at the end of a particularly artful sentence. "I'll ride with you, how about. That way if something goes wrong, we'll both be maimed."

"I—" That stops me. On one hand, I fully believe I'm inviting grievous bodily injury—or worse—by climbing into that broken-down hunk of junk. On the other, smashed into a confined space with Clayton Carville would be the very definition of a good death. Without entirely meaning to, I imagine Dr. Paula Prescott dressed in '80s-style play clothes—a Day-Glo tank top and high tops, maybe—strolling the grounds of the Douglas Fair.

"Okay," I hear myself say. "Let's go."

"Really?" Carrie looks flabbergasted.

"Yep." I offer a tight-lipped smile and a single nod. "Quick," I tell them, leading the way through the crowd in the direction of my own impending doom, "before I change my mind."

The line is short, so I don't have time to reconsider or chicken out before all at once the zitty, frowning ride operator straps me and Clayton into our seats. It's a small car, the sides of our thighs pressing together; his bare knee just barely brushes mine as he wraps his hands around the safety bar and glances in my direction. "You okay?" he asks, smirking a little.

"Um, yup," I manage. In truth I'm barely breathing, though I'd be hard pressed to say whether it's because we're about to be launched into the air like a spitball and then free fall back toward the pavement or because the side of Clayton's pinky is brushing the side of mine.

He nods, then takes a deep breath. "Listen," he says. "About the party last night—"

That's when the latch goes loose, and suddenly there's nothing above us except sky.

At first all the noises in the world—the joyful squeals of little kids on the Tilt-A-Whirl, the bratwurst hawker shouting about his deals, the rhythmic *ding* of the ring toss game—all of it fades away to silence. There's just me sitting here next to Clayton, hardly even registering our high-speed ascent as I wonder desperately what he was about to say.

I can hear my heart thumping as we reach the apex, the sound of blood swishing wildly through my body; then we start to fall, and it's drowned out by something much, much louder. It's only a second before I realize it's *also* coming from me: I'm screaming, wild and ragged, from an inside deeper than I knew I had. The gravitational pull pushes me against the seat so I can't turn my head, but from the corner of my eye I can tell Clayton is laughing; after a moment I'm laughing too as we launch back up again.

This ricochet pattern, screaming then laughing, flying then falling, continues a few more times before we slow and then come to a suspended stop. I'm still clutching the bar when the attendant comes to unlatch us. It's only when I look down that I notice Clayton and my fingers are overlapping now, his hand on top of mine.

He pulls his back, wiping his palms on the front of his khaki shorts before reaching out again, his grip warm and steadying as I climb out of the Ejector car. My legs feel like water. My brain is full of gauze. "So?" he asks, waving at Carrie and Ethan as the attendant straps them in for their turn. "Want to go again?"

"No way," I say, and I mean it. But the truth is I'm glad I tried it once.

✳

Carrie's mystery man shows up just as we're finishing with the Ejector—this guy Adam Meyers I remember from elementary school, when he used to try to convince everyone to play Pokémon at recess every day and carried a backpack in the shape of a monkey's face until we were way too old for that kind of thing to be socially acceptable. He transferred to Hartwick Prep in ninth grade—his family made a billion dollars on a chain of local department stores and presumably wanted him to learn to speak dead languages and, like, be rude to service people, or whatever it is they teach you at private school—but I have to admit the years have not exactly been unkind to him. "Adam Meyers got *extremely* cute," I whisper to Carrie as we amble along the midway.

"Ugh, I know," she says, wrinkling her nose like "got extremely cute" is synonymous with "still wets the bed" or "was never vaccinated for any childhood diseases because his parents don't trust the government." "It's the worst."

I laugh, the two of us hanging back as the guys stop off at the free-throw booth, all of them loudly impugning one another's basketball skills. "Why is it the worst?" Adam keeps glancing back at Carrie like he thinks he's being slick, and I think of a recent cross-word clue: *Trash talk from the peacock with the best courtship display.* Twelve letters.

Tailgloating.

Carrie sighs. "I mean, we all know *you* love yourself a preppy white boy," she says, shooting a meaningful look in Clayton's direction as he hands a couple of dollars over to the carnie running the game, "but some of us have reputations to maintain."

She's teasing me again, familiar, but this time I don't smile. "Wait, *what?*" I look from her to the boys, back again. Does everybody know how I feel about Clayton? Does *Clayton* know how I feel about Clayton? Ugh, this right here is exactly why I never leave my house. "I don't—"

"Suck it, Carville!" Ethan crows, doing a corny victory dance on the dusty midway as the barker hands over a giant stuffed giraffe.

We hang out at the fair for a while longer, eating deep-fried Snickers bars and riding the Scrambler—in that order, actually, which is probably ill-advised—but the truth is I'm not having that much fun anymore. I feel out of sorts and exposed, an animal showing its raw pink belly. There's a part of me that wishes I'd just hung out with Miles tonight instead, watching *The Last Jedi* in his basement and eating cheese balls out of the tub. By the time Adam asks if we want to go meet up with a bunch of his friends at a party in town, all I want to do is go home.

"I've actually got to head out," I tell Carrie, who's looking at me hopefully. She feels bad about what she said about me and Clayton, I can tell. "You should go, though."

"What? No way," she protests, looking from me to Adam and back again. "I'm not going to just ditch you here. How are you even going to get home?"

"I'll call somebody," I promise. Maybe it's not too late for Mom and I to swing by Moxie's after all, though the idea of any more sugar makes me feel a little sick. "It's totally fine."

"I can take her," Clayton interjects from right behind me—and crap, how long has he been standing there? He hasn't had two words for me since we got off the Ejector, like possibly the jolting of the ride reconnected some circuit in his brain and he remembered he didn't have anything to say after all.

Carrie's dark eyes light up. "Are you sure?" she asks him, then frowns a little. "Like, do you even know where she lives?"

Clayton laughs. "I think between the two of us we can probably figure it out." He turns to me, raises his eyebrows. "That work for you?"

My heart is turning over in spite of itself, but I force a shrug. "Yeah," I say, tucking my hands into my pockets and rocking back on the heels of my sneakers. *It's just a ride home,* I remind myself firmly. It doesn't mean anything. "That works for me."

Clayton drives the kind of giant, hulking SUV that announces to the world you're a person who's never needed to worry about gas money, the passenger seat so high it takes me a minute to clamber awkwardly inside. It's way cleaner than I think of boys' cars as being, with an air freshener clipped to the air vent and a plastic bag slung over the gear shift for collecting garbage. When he turns on the engine, the satellite radio is programmed to Prime Country, which surprises me; it's the same corny station we're always teasing my dad for liking, all George Strait and Alan Jackson songs from way back before I was born. "Sorry," Clayton says, jabbing at the display screen until he gets to the Top 40 station. When I glance over at him in the greenish glow of the dashboard lights, I can see that he's blushing. "Now you know my secret shame."

"Oh yeah, you're a real deviant," I tell him with a smile. "Next thing you're going to tell me you've got a Trisha Yearwood poster hanging above your bed."

"See, you're kidding right now, but I actually have every single episode of her cooking show saved on my DVR."

I snort, feeling myself relax a little. "You do not."

"No, I seriously do."

"Your celebrity crush is Trisha *Yearwood*?"

"Trisha Yearwood is American royalty, Rachel."

"I apologize," I say with a giggle that surprises me. "Obviously what you two have is very special."

"Thank you." Clayton glances over at me, winking as we pull out of the fairgrounds and onto the service road that leads to the highway. This area is pretty rural, that thick Michigan blackness pressing in on all sides. "So," he says after a moment, "I didn't know you and Carrie were friends."

"Oh. Well, we used to be," I say, glancing down and picking at a cuticle. "Until high school."

"Really? What happened?"

I shrug. "Nothing, really. Sometimes people just change, you know?"

"You or her?"

"Both of us," I lie.

Clayton nods as we pull onto the highway. "Fair enough," he murmurs, almost to himself. For a moment I wonder if maybe he's not talking about me and Carrie at all. I think again of him and Bethany on the shore of the creek the other night, the resolute *snick* of the bedroom door at Spencer's.

"Anyway," I continue, "we started talking again last night, and . . ." I trail off. I don't want it to sound like I'm fishing, bringing up the party again, even if the reality is I'm dying to get back to whatever he was going to say before the Ejector cranked to terrifying life. *What are you* doing *with me?* I want to ask him. *What do you even want?*

"About that, PS," Clayton says, reaching out and turning the stereo down a click, "I think I probably owe you an apology."

"What, for last night?" I ask, playing dumb, which even I know is ridiculous. "Why?"

"For, like, asking you to come and then being totally MIA the whole time." He makes a face. "It's complicated with Bethany, that's all."

"Don't worry about it," I tell him, wanting to play it off like I imagine a cool girl would. *Who, me? I hardly even noticed you weren't there, I was so busy being chill and popular!* "Relationships are hard."

I think it's a very mature thing to say, considering I have had exactly zero relationships in my life from which to draw such a sage conclusion, but right away Clayton shakes his head. "No no, it's not like that," he says, his tone definitive. "We're not together."

My heart stops beating entirely, just for one second. "You're not?"

"I mean, we *were*," he says, "obviously. Up until a couple months ago. But not anymore."

I dig my fingernails into my palms, barely holding back a flood of intrusive questions. *What happened?* I'm dying to ask him. *What's complicated about it? If you're broken up, why are there still so many pictures of you guys together on Instagram?* "That's too bad" is all I say.

"It's not," Clayton says flatly. "I love Bethany—she's one of my best friends—but. Yeah. It's for the best." He rubs at his neck for a moment, like there's a muscle bothering him there. "Anyway, I invited you last night because I wanted you to come."

I think of what Carrie said, about him not being the kind of person who does anything by accident. "You did?" I can't help but ask.

Clayton smiles at that, just faintly. "Yeah, Rach," he says, and just for a second he sounds shyer than I've ever heard him. "I don't know. You seem like the kind of person who's worth putting in the work to get to know."

Holy shit. "Well, joke's on you." Even as the words come out I can hear Nonna telling me not to put myself down, but it's like my brain can't process the compliment, especially from someone like Clayton. "I'm actually super boring."

Clayton glances at me sidelong. "Somehow I doubt that."

"You really shouldn't."

"Okay," he concedes, laughing a little. "Fair enough. Boring like what, exactly? Your hobbies include watching paint dry and your favorite food is dry toast?"

I think about that. "Boring like . . . I've basically spent the last four years in a holding pattern, I guess? Like I've been waiting for my life to actually, finally start. But what I'm starting to figure out is that all that time, there was all this stuff I was actually missing out on."

"Meaning . . . ?"

I try to think of a way to explain it that isn't *I badly want to make out with you.* "Well, for example. My nonna got me a suitcase and a passport for my sixteenth birthday, and that year, I was supposed to go on the France trip at school. But my friend Ruoxi ended up getting mono and couldn't go, so I backed out at the last minute. Because I didn't want to go alone."

Clayton nods, glancing in the rearview mirror. "That was a good trip."

I elbow him across the gearshift. "Yes, thank you. I gathered that." I followed it obsessively on Instagram and Snapchat, I remember, sitting in my room thousands of miles away as my classmates—as

Clayton and Bethany—climbed the Eiffel Tower and mugged in front of the *Mona Lisa* and ate croissants on the banks of the Seine. "Anyway, here I am, almost two years later and I've still never been to France. I don't even have a stamp in my passport yet."

"Okay," Clayton says. "I hear you. For what it's worth, though, I'd say you have your whole life to fill up with experiences. It's not over yet." He looks over and smiles at me then, easy and familiar and *private*. I shiver without being able to help it—the full-body thrill of being here alone in this car with him, being the object of his attention even if it's only for a little while.

"You cold?" Clayton asks.

"Um, a little," I lie, because it's less embarrassing than the truth.

"Here," he says, reaching back with one hand and rooting around behind the passenger seat before coming up with a zip-up hoodie appliqued with some kind of bird.

"Is that a . . . chicken?" I ask, sliding my arms into the sleeves. The cotton smells like him, a combination of dryer sheets, sunscreen, and citrus.

Clayton laughs. "It's the Hotspurs," he explains.

"I'm . . . going to pretend like I know what that means."

"It's a football club," he tells me. "Soccer, I mean. In Tottenham? London? They're in the Premier League."

"Oh, right!" I exclaim a bit too excitedly. "Sports!"

"Possibly the only form of entertainment I care about more than Trisha Yearwood," he says with a smile. "I'm guessing you're not a sports person, huh?"

"We all have our skill sets," I say primly. "Athleticism is not one of mine."

"Soccer is mostly a game of strategy," Clayton counters. "The thinking person's sport. You might like it."

Oh, I'm fully going to go home and Google stats on every player until I know them better than my own family, I think. "Maybe I'll give it a shot."

Clayton nods. "You should."

We're pulling off the highway now, not far from my neighborhood; it feels like my time with him is running out. *I want to put the work in to get to know you too,* I want to tell him. *I've wanted that for a long time.*

Instead I reach forward and press a finger to the screen on the dashboard as Clayton stops at a red light, flipping through the satellite stations until I get back to Prime Country. I'm hoping for Trisha Yearwood, but instead it's a Brooks & Dunn song I don't recognize. Still, Clayton looks over at me with an expression I don't know him well enough to read, exactly. It is *not,* if I had to guess, the expression of a person who isn't interested in seeing me again after tonight.

He reaches forward and turns up the volume. Up above us, the stoplight turns green.

7

*M*iles and I set out with the Cream Cart at noon the following day, the two of us parked on the boardwalk in our matching DiPasquale's T-shirts as tourists sun themselves like lizards on the sand. Every summer, our small coastal Michigan town swells with tourists, most of them from Illinois and all of them vying for a spot on the ten miles of freshwater beachfront. A half hour into our shift we've already sold a third of our inventory, people lining up faster than Miles can scoop gelato. Dad's idea really is genius.

A cloud passes in front of the sun as the breeze lifts off the water, and I reach for Clayton's hoodie even though it's still way too warm. I realized after he dropped me off last night that I was still holding it—all right, I fully stole it right out of his car like a common thief—and I decided to bring it with me today in case I happened to see him around.

You know, like a normal person would.

Totally low key.

OMG what! Ruoxi texts back after I tell her what happened. By all accounts she's having an amazing time at Interlochen, sending me Snaps of her blistered fingers and her knee socks and Clarissa, the cello player from Westport she's got a massive crush on. **That's amazing!**

I send her the upside-down smiling emoji, then tuck my phone back into the pocket of my shorts.

"So," Miles says, handing two Stracciatella Gondolas to a hassled-looking mom with a couple of whining kids hanging off her, "what's up with the jacket?"

"Huh?" I glance down, like I've hardly even noticed I'm wearing it. "Oh. It's the Tottenham Hotspurs."

"Yes," Miles says with a smirk, "I see that. Where'd you get it?"

"I . . . borrowed it," I tell him, which is technically not a lie. "From a friend."

Miles raises an eyebrow, wiping a smear of gelato from the tiny prep counter. "A friend who's into soccer?"

It's his *You have no usual crew* voice, and I prickle. "How do you know the Hotspurs are a soccer team?"

"I know plenty of things," Miles says with a shrug. "I just don't care about them."

"Oh, right, I forgot." I smile cheerily at an old couple strolling by in matching fanny packs, then let it drop as soon as they've passed. "You're too cool for any kind of enthusiasm."

He tilts his head, a lock of dark hair falling into his face. "I mean,

I wouldn't go *that* far," he amends, his voice dripping with innuendo. "I can be very enthusiastic, when the situation demands it."

"Okay, okay." I jam a handful of napkins into the dispenser. "It's Clayton's."

That surprises him. "Clayton *Carville*?"

"Yup," I say, popping the *p* like a chewing gum bubble and feeling extremely satisfied with myself. Is this what it's like to be a popular person? The ability to walk around sticking it to your annoying childhood sidekick whenever you want?

Miles certainly *looks* like my childhood sidekick all of a sudden, that's for sure, all the smirking guile wiped right off his face. "Seriously?" he asks, his voice cracking like I haven't heard it do since we were twelve. "You're trading clothes with Clayton Carville."

"I mean, I don't think he's wearing any of mine," I say snottily. Then I shrug. "It's a new development."

Miles looks at me for a moment, an expression I don't recognize passing across his face like a cloud. If it wasn't totally demented to contemplate, I'd say he looks almost . . . wounded. Then he blinks, and just like that he's himself again, his features twisting dismissively. "Well," he says, "I hope you kids are very happy together."

Suddenly there's a loud clanking noise, diverting our attention to the freezer. "What's that?" I ask with a wince.

Miles makes an *I don't know* sound. He turns and flips the cooler switch on and then off again, the motor whizzing for a second before stalling out. He frowns at it for another moment, waves his hand over the hole of the freezing bin. "The cooling mechanism maybe?" he diagnoses finally. "I think it just shit the bed."

"Evocative," I say drily. "Can you fix it?"

"Do I look like an ice cream cart mechanic to you?" he deadpans. "We definitely can't keep opening the container like this, though. The air won't stay cold enough to keep the gelato from melting."

I bite my lip. This is not good. Business at DiPasquale's is fine these days, but right now I can feel the anxiety of the precarious months right after we opened running through me, my parents bent worriedly over paperwork at the kitchen table and vendor invoices marked PAST DUE. We were on food stamps when I was a baby, a fact I know my mom thinks I don't remember. Every item of clothing I owned came from Goodwill or Nonna until I was ten. Money isn't a joke to me, and my dad spent a lot of it on this cream cart. The idea of it breaking down on literally the first day makes me feel like I can't breathe. "Miles, we have to fix it."

I must look about two scoops short of a sundae, because Miles's whole demeanor shifts when he glances over and sees the expression on my face. "Okay, okay," he says, scratching the back of his neck and considering the cooler. "Easy. Let me think for a sec."

He taps the thing with his foot, flipping the switch a few more times. Now the fan doesn't whirr at all. "Well, that didn't do anything." His gaze flicks from me to the line of customers that's formed while we've been standing here debating, all of them beginning to murmur impatiently. "Folks, we have to take a quick break," he announces, holding up a conciliatory hand to the beachgoers. "Technical difficulties."

I turn to stare at him, unable to keep the incredulous smile off my face in spite of the way my heart is pounding. "I'm sorry," I tell him, "did you just say *folks*?"

Miles ignores me. "Stay here," he instructs, sounding more authoritative than I've ever heard him. "I'll be back in a sec."

I scrawl a makeshift "gone fishing" sign on the chalkboard menu and plop down on the boardwalk beside the Cream Cart, picking at a loose thread on Clayton's hoodie while I wait for Miles to return. I can't help but wonder what his reaction was about earlier, how weird he seemed about the idea of me and Clayton hanging out. Yeah, Miles likes to torment me. But he doesn't mean anything by it.

Right?

After another fifteen minutes, Miles reappears with a tool belt that definitely does not belong to him.

"Where did you get that?" I ask, getting to my feet and brushing off the back of my shorts.

"Tommy's buddy Jon owed me a favor," he explains, gesturing toward the bike rental place a quarter mile up the beach. "I rebuilt his processor a year or so ago."

"Like his computer?" I ask, impressed in spite of myself. Miles acts like such a burnout sometimes that it's easy to forget he could probably run NASA if he could be bothered to get out of bed before noon.

"Yeah, like his computer." Miles shrugs. "This isn't the same thing, obviously, but I feel like it can't be that different either. Most machines have a fan to keep them from overheating. I think if I can get that grate off and take a look inside, I can probably figure it out."

My eyes widen. "Really?"

"Sure," Miles says in a voice that suggests he's less confident than he's trying to convince me he is. "What's the worst that can happen?"

"I mean, you could make it worse."

"Well . . . true, technically." Miles grins. "But I have a good feeling about this."

He gets to work, lying down on the boardwalk and wriggling underneath the Cream Cart, his lower body sticking out like the Wicked Witch of the West in *The Wizard of Oz*. His T-shirt has rucked up the tiniest bit, the elastic waistband of his Calvin Klein boxer-briefs just visible where it's sticking out of his jeans. I turn away, looking out at the beach and trying not to wonder if his mom still buys his underwear or if he went into a store and purchased them himself. I wouldn't have pegged him for a designer boxer-brief kind of guy.

I mean, not that I spend a lot of time thinking about Miles's underwear or anything.

Because I don't.

He grunts a couple times, muttering unintelligibly to himself, and then finally I hear a clank. "Okay," he calls, his voice muffled. "Now try the switch."

When I flip it, the machine whirrs to life, humming along like normal in a matter of seconds. "Holy crap," I say, laughing in spite of myself. When he scoots out from underneath the Cream Cart, I hold out a hand to help him up. "That actually *worked*?"

Miles snorts. "Try not to die from shock," he says, brushing his hands off.

"I kind of love you a little bit right now, I won't lie."

"You love me all the time," he says automatically, though the tips of his ears are pinking up a little bit and I don't think it's from the sun. "We'll have to be careful when we bring this thing onto the beach," he continues, looking at the Cream Cart speculatively. "Can't get sand in it." He scrubs a hand through his messy hair. "Maybe I can find some mesh screen to put over the fan or something."

"Miles Vandenberg." I pop up on my tiptoes, pretending to feel his forehead for a fever. "Are you sick? You're actually going out of your way to help someone? Look at you, being a decent human."

"Yeah, yeah." He bumps my shoulder with his, then turns back to the Cream Cart. "Don't get used to it."

We sell out of Gondolas within the hour, the line so long and unrelenting we barely have time to talk. By the time we close up shop for the day, I've got gelato dried into the creases of my elbows and Miles is complaining about the strain on his scooping arm. "So we should head back to DiPasquale's, then?" he asks, dumping some bottled water onto a paper napkin and handing it to me so that I can clean up.

"Thanks," I say, surprised by the gesture. We should get back, I guess—at some point we have to return the cart so it's ready to be stocked for tomorrow—but the restaurant is fully staffed. Dad hired a couple new people to make up for the fact that Miles and I are on the beach this summer and leaving in August, so it's not like there's any hurry. Why not just enjoy the rest of the afternoon? "I might just . . . hang out."

Miles's eyes widen. "Really?" he asks. "Is that a thing you do?"

I snort. "Yes?"

"I don't know," Miles says. "Don't you have, like, some pre-collegiate enrichment classes you need to get back to? Or, like, some nursing home residents to go sing to in Spanish?"

"Oh, you're hilarious." I throw the damp wad of napkins at him. "Why do people always say that?" I ask. "I like fun! I like hanging out! And for the record, I did that nursing home thing *one time* and it's probably what got me into Northwestern."

"Uh-huh." Miles doesn't bother hiding his smirk. "And what kind of fun did you have in mind, exactly?"

That stops me. "I mean, I didn't have a *plan*."

"Oh, I see." Miles nods seriously. "It's spontaneous fun you're after."

"Exactly."

He digs his phone out of his pocket, scrolls for a moment. "We could go to a movie," he offers. "They're showing *Jaws* at the dollar theater in twenty minutes."

I raise my eyebrows, goading. "Oh, now you're intending to have this fun *with* me, I see."

I'm teasing, but Miles doesn't smile. "I mean, not if you don't want me to," he says immediately, and I roll my eyes.

"Oh, don't be such a whiny little diaper baby." I shake my head, looking out at the wide expanse of beach, the deep blue sky up above. It's warm but not oppressively, the heat a pleasant prickle on my skin. "It's too nice for a movie," I decide. "We should, like, play outside."

"Oh yeah?" Miles's shoulders drop, his whole body seeming to relax at my use of the first-person plural. "What, you want to go find some monkey bars?"

"I mean, kind of," I admit. It's not the worst idea he's ever had. "But I was actually thinking about a hike."

"A hike?" He looks at me dubiously. "You?"

"Haven't you heard?" I ask, smiling sweetly. "I'm trying new things."

"Yeah, so I gather." Miles rolls his shoulders, like he's trying to get limbered up. Back in elementary school, he was the only person in our entire class who hated gym class more than me. "And where exactly is this alleged hike going to occur?"

I consider that. "I mean, we could always go to Mount Bald—"

"No. Don't say it." Miles groans.

"Mount Baldhead." Mount Baldhead is this ridiculous dune not far from here, with a man-made staircase that you can climb to get the most amazing view of both Kalamazoo Lake and Lake Michigan. "It's only three hundred stairs, Mi. You can do it. Or not. No one is forcing you to come."

"Three hundred and two, actually. And the last two are the hardest."

"Uh-huh." I shake my head. "Again, you don't have to—"

"I want to," Miles interrupts roughly, his dark gaze catching mine, and suddenly neither one of us is kidding around anymore. "Okay? I want to."

I swallow hard, bending down to scoop the napkin off the ground and tossing it into the trash. "Okay, then," I say once I'm upright again, my voice coming out a tiny bit strangled. "Let's go."

He grins, snapping whatever weird invisible thread was just stretching between us. "I mean, you're going to have to carry my lifeless body back down the mountain when I pass out and die on you," he warns me, "but don't worry: I'm sure the good people at Northwestern will find that very impressive as well."

※

When we reach Mount Baldhead, I lock up the cart and double-check the padlocks on the cooler compartments. There's nothing left inside, but I don't want anyone messing with it. I grab my backpack and start for the steps while Miles tosses his head back and takes a few deep breaths, psyching himself up. "All right," he says finally, making a big show of reaching his arms over his head and executing a couple of corny aerobics-instructor stretches. "Let's do this."

I'm hardly in what you'd call peak physical condition—I don't think I've run anywhere since our neighbor's corgi, Jamie Oliver, got loose in the neighborhood last fall—but Miles wasn't kidding. He makes me look like the kind of person who'd do a Tough Mudder for fun. We're on the fifth landing when he holds a hand up to stop me: "Ahhh," he wheezes, bending over and pressing his palms against his knees, "I am. Out of. Shape."

"Miles!" I chide, handing him my water bottle. "We've still got like two hundred steps to go."

"Two hundred and twenty-two," he corrects, downing half my water before passing it back and wiping his mouth with the back of one wrist, "but who's counting?"

On the way up, we get passed by two grandmas in orthopedic running shoes and fanny packs, and a short while later, by a troop of high school kids who are clearly teams in training. Miles takes the opportunity to pause against the railing as they pass. His breathing is less labored, but his face is pink with exertion. On one hand, I'm a little worried he wasn't kidding about needing me to haul him back down the mountain.

On the other, damp and sweaty isn't a *bad* look on him, exactly.

Gah. What is my problem? Am I seriously so starved for human affection that I've resorted to perving on *Miles,* of all people? Who's next? Jackson's little roller-hockey friends?

"Are you seriously okay?" I ask, my voice coming out more irritated than I intend in my attempt to cover. "Because if you're about to hurl—"

"I'm fine," Miles says, sounding equally peeved. "Sorry we can't all be national youth soccer stars, or whatever."

"Wait, *what?*" I whirl to look at him. "What does *that* mean?"

"Forget it," he says immediately. "Come on, let's go."

"No," I counter, planting my feet and staying right where I am. "Are you talking about Clayton?"

"I'm not talking about anybody," Miles says. "I'm being an asshole." He shakes his head, softening a little. "Seriously. Let's just get to the top, okay?"

I frown, weirdly unwilling to drop it. It doesn't make any sense: Miles has never shown any real interest in me, not in all the time we've known each other. What does he care if I hang out with Clayton?

"Fine," I say at last, not sure how to press him without making it sound like something I know it probably isn't. "Let's go."

We take the last five flights slowly, neither of us saying anything. The view from the top is just as incredible as I remember, water stretching out in every direction, all that endless sky. I hand my water bottle to Miles wordlessly; he takes another long gulp, his Adam's apple moving inside his throat as he drinks. "I used to come up here with my brother," he announces, handing it back.

I blink, one because it's the first thing either of us has said in twenty minutes, and two because—cool-guy act notwithstanding— Miles never talks about Tommy. Like, not ever. Hearing his name twice in one day feels like falling into an alternate dimension.

I bite my lip for a moment before responding, feeling like I'm trying not to startle a rare bird out of the palm of my hand. "Oh yeah?" I ask finally, finishing the last of the water. I'm sure it's mostly backwash by now, which should probably gross me out more than it does.

"Yeah." Miles nods. "We used to race each other to the top. Last one up had to do the other one's chores for a week, that kind of thing."

I raise an eyebrow, teasing. "You did this voluntarily?"

"I mean, no," Miles says with a laugh. "Tommy was the boss of me; you know that. He used to make me do it because he was bigger and knew he could kick my ass." He takes a deep breath and grabs the railing, shaking it a little like he's checking to make sure it'll hold. "The last time I came up here was the night he died."

It feels like the Cream Cart breaking down all over again, some important whirring piece of machinery grinding to a sudden stop deep inside me. "Crap, Miles," I say, almost taking a step toward him and then thinking better of it. "I'm sorry. If I'd known, I—"

"I could have bailed," Miles cuts me off. "And I didn't." He shrugs. "Besides, it's not like I magically don't think about him if I'm not up here or something. I think about him all the effing time."

"No, of course, but . . ." I trail off. I guess I never really thought about it, how every place Miles goes is probably a place he went with Tommy at some point, his brother's ghost lurking around every corner of town. Most of the time Miles's *I'm Impervious to All Human Emotions* act is so convincing that it's easy to forget that of course he isn't, that he didn't just mourn his brother or whatever and then immediately shut that part of himself off for the rest of eternity. "You miss him?" I ask, which is an extremely stupid question. But all Miles does is nod.

"Yeah," he says, abandoning the view and heading for a nearby patch of grass, facing away from me so I almost don't hear him. "Every day."

He flops down onto the ground and I ease myself down beside him, tilting my face up and closing my eyes so the sun makes swirling patterns on the backs of my eyelids. "I told you those last two steps are the hardest," he informs me.

I kick him in the ankle to reply.

8

*M*om is making pancakes when I come downstairs to the kitchen the next morning, Jackson shoving them into his face basically as fast as they come off the griddle. "Save some for your sister, will you?" Nonna chides as I pour myself a cup of coffee. Jackson stuffs another one into his mouth in reply.

"Where's Dad?" I ask. The puzzles page of the paper is folded so that the crossword is neatly displayed; its organized squares are tidy and blank.

"Errands to run," Mom explains, handing me a plate before ladling some more batter into her frying pan, the smell of melting butter and maple syrup filling the air. I plunk myself down at the table just as my phone buzzes inside the kangaroo pocket of my hoodie. **So,** reads the text, which comes from a local number that's not in my contacts list, **what new life experiences are on the docket today?**

I frown. **Sorry,** I type. **Who is this?**

Guess.

I set my mug down on the table, my entire body suddenly on alert. The truth is there's only one person I've talked to about my little project whose number isn't already programmed into my phone. It couldn't be . . .

Could it?

No idea, I type finally, hedging. No reason to embarrass myself more than absolutely necessary. **Can I get a hint?**

Well, comes the reply a moment later. **I'm pretty sure you made off with my Hotspurs hoodie the other night.**

Holy *shit.* I almost fall right out of my chair, all shock and embarrassment and a warm, unfamiliar pleasure. Clayton freaking *Carville,* going out of his way to ask around for my number. Texting me completely unprovoked.

Even if it is to accuse me of being a petty criminal.

OMG, I type, **I'm so sorry! I didn't even realize I had it until you were gone.**

A likely story, Clayton writes back, plus the chin-stroking emoji. Then, a moment later: **So what's the plan for today?**

Working the Cream Cart with Miles and watching *The Great British Bake Off* with Nonna, most likely, but I'm not about to tell that to Clayton. **Oh, you know. Considering a hot-air balloon ride. Jetting off to Europe, perhaps.**

Gotta get that virgin passport stamped, he agrees.

I blink, a delicious little thrill ricocheting through me. It sounds

like one of Miles's cheesy come-ons, except for the part where it's
from Clayton and it's basically the most exciting text I've ever received in my life. I mean, no *basically* about it; it *is* the most exciting
text I've ever received in my life. I can't believe I'm still sitting here
at my kitchen table while my brother hoovers pancakes into his
maw and Nonna flips through the paper, complaining about the
town council being run by a bunch of Republican fascists. It feels
like I should have projected to a higher astral plane.

Exactly. I take a sip of my sweet, milky coffee, enjoying myself
now. **Can't be wasting time.**

You realize Canada is only five hours from here.

Ha, I type. **We should go.**

Clayton doesn't reply for a moment—which, shit, was that over
the line? I frown at the screen, watching as the little blue thought
bubble appears, then goes away again. I'm about to reassure him I'm
only kidding when the three dots show up one more time; then, a
second later:

Can you be ready in an hour?

Lol, I type back, fully thinking he's kidding. **Sure. What do you
need for Canada, bear repellant and a Mountie uniform?**

I'm serious.

I sit up straighter in my chair—glancing over at my mom, who's
humming the jingle from a local tire shop commercial while she
finishes up with the pancakes. **Wait, really?**

Why not?

I can think of a million reasons why not, actually: I have to work today, first of all. My parents would freak the hell out. And, despite the fact that I've been carrying on a torrid and passionate mental affair with Clayton for the better part of four full years now, we don't actually know each other.

Like, at all.

I'm about to make up some kind of excuse when a picture pops into my head of Dr. Paula in '80s-style traveling clothes—big sunglasses and a car coat, maybe, a flowered scarf wrapped around her massive perm.

Just say yes, right?

An hour works, I type, fully unable to believe this is actually happening. **You're in charge of snacks.**

※

An hour is long enough for the house to clear out, thank goodness, Jackson off to camp and my mom to the restaurant to do some prep work, Nonna heading off to the senior center for her twice-weekly Zumba class. Once they're gone, I scroll through my phone until I get to Miles's name: **Hey,** I text, **must have overdone it on our hike yesterday. Feeling like trash. You good to cover the Cream Cart this afternoon?**

His reply comes fast: **Will do. You need anything?**

I blink, surprised by the offer. **Nope, I'm good. Try not to make any little kids cry.**

Where's the fun in that?

I jump in the shower before spending twenty precious minutes digging through my closet in search of some outfit that's (a) cute, (b) not too try-hard, and (c) appropriate for an international excursion with the literal guy of my dreams. I own exactly zero items of clothing that fit that description, however, so in the end I wriggle into my favorite jeans and a navy-and-white striped tank top, braiding my long hair into a rope over one shoulder and attempting a mostly unsuccessful eyeliner application. I'm just flossing my teeth—look, I'm not saying there's going to be kissing on this trip, but if there is, I am certainly not about to be brought down by imperfect oral hygiene—when Clayton texts to say he's outside.

I bound down the stairs so fast I almost break an ankle, pausing in the foyer to collect myself before swinging the front door open. He's parked in the driveway in his giant SUV, looking effortlessly adorable in a pair of khaki shorts and a rumpled blue T-shirt. Somehow, I suspect he didn't floss. There are two iced coffees sweating in the cupholders, a reusable grocery tote on the floor of the passenger seat bulging with a whole concession stand's worth of chips and candy.

"I didn't know what you liked, so I just got all my favorites and hoped for the best," he explains. "Ready to go?"

I grin, my heart expanding like an overfull balloon inside my rib cage. "Yes."

※

Five hours in the car is a long time with anyone, let alone the object of my true and undying affection, and I'm terrified it's going to be awkward, but actually Clayton is weirdly easy to talk to: about working at the restaurant; about Marquette, where he's headed in the fall; about his little sister Ruthie, who's got a pretty lucrative side hustle making friendship bracelets and selling them in an Etsy shop. "I was wondering where you'd gotten that," I say, nodding at the one looped around his wrist—thick and intricately knotted, woven in shades of blue and green.

"Oh, no," Clayton deadpans. "This one I made myself."

Still, we run out of steam about an hour in, just the wind blowing in through the open windows and the twang of Reba McEntire on Prime Country. I try to take in the scenery out the window—Michigan is stupidly beautiful this time of year, the trees on either side of the highway a million brilliant adjectives beyond green—but I can't help but be a little more interested in the view inside the car. I spent so long watching Clayton from across the cafeteria or through a computer screen that it feels almost unnatural to be this close to him, like I'm on safari and paid extra to have the animals stick their heads inside the Jeep. His eyelashes are blonder than the hair on his head, I notice; there's a tiny scar on the side of his chin, the shape of a crescent moon.

Clayton shifts around in his seat, digging his phone out of his pocket and passing it to me. "Here," he says. "Want to pick a podcast or something? Pin is 3141."

I blink, shocked by how easily he handed it over. My own phone is a fortress of embarrassing Google searches and screenshots of other people's Instagram stories preserved for further perusal; I'd rather throw the thing into Lake Michigan than give anyone else the code. "Uh, I'm sorry," I say as I key in the digits. His background is a photo of the entire soccer team—Clayton's arms draped around the shoulders of a couple other guys I recognize, all of them sweaty and muddy and smiling. "Is your phone password the first four digits of pi?"

Clayton grins. "Busted," he says. "You know you're the only person who's ever picked up on that?"

I feel my cheeks warm, dorkily pleased. "Yeah, well, I'm a nerd."

"Me too, evidently."

My lips twist, all skepticism. "Mmm, doubtful." I click on his podcasts app, fully expecting to have to feign enthusiasm for *The Best of Barstool Sports* in the name of love, but I'm surprised to find an assortment of options, ranging from sciencey stuff to the latest NPR whodunit to American history and government. "Okay," I concede, clicking on one called *[environ]Mental*. "Maybe you are kind of a secret nerd."

"I'm saying!" Clayton laughs as the tinkling theme music plays. "These dudes are super interesting, though. They go all around the country exploring the aftermath of major environmental disasters that have these massive implications, but that basically no one has ever heard of or remembers. Except, obviously, the people who live near them and whose kids are, like, being born with gills and fins."

We listen in silence for a few minutes as the hosts explain about an eighty-four-acre solid waste containment area where a dike ruptured, spilling over a billion gallons of coal ash slurry into the surrounding area. It *is* interesting, in a horrifying kind of way. Most of all I like the way Clayton listens: head tilted to the side in concentration, swearing under his breath at the worst, most infuriating parts. Usually I'm the one geeking out over stuff, getting worked up about minutiae nobody else seems to care about. It's kind of nice to see someone else do it.

"So this is something you're interested in?" I ask during a chipper, slightly manic-sounding commercial for a smoothie-delivery program.

"What?" Clayton asks, glancing over his shoulder and changing lanes as a giant truck blows by us. "Podcasts?"

"No, like, the environment. Our rapidly heating planet, the inevitable breakdown of civilization as we know it." I smile brightly. "You know, fun stuff like that."

"I am, yeah." He nods. "Really interested, actually. I'm going to Marquette because of the soccer scholarship, but I picked it over a couple other options mostly because they have a pretty great environmental studies program."

"Oh, wow," I say. "Okay, so you're like, *really* interested, then."

"Yeah," Clayton says. "I mean, I don't know what I want to do with it exactly, but I figure I'll have time to work it out."

I think of what Carrie said the other night, about the Art Institute. Neither of them has the future all planned, but it doesn't seem to bother them. It must be sort of liberating—that is, along with being terrifying and probably ill-advised. "So soccer isn't a long-term thing?"

He laughs. "You mean be a professional soccer player? Uh, no."

"I don't know!" I laugh too, embarrassed. "I have no idea how professional sports work. You're good at soccer, are you not?"

"Not that good," Clayton says firmly. "Plus, like, you have to really love it."

"And you don't?"

Clayton hesitates. "It's not that I don't, exactly. But not enough for it to be my whole life. And also, like . . . I don't know." He chews the corner of his lip. "Sometimes I wonder, like . . ."

"What?" I prod, knowing even as the word comes out of my mouth that I sound a full click too eager. *Confide in me,* I want to tell him. *I promise I'm a person you can trust.*

"I don't know," Clayton says again. "Just, like, if I wasn't this guy—Soccer Dude, or whatever—would anybody still give a shit about me?"

"You mean, like, would you still be the actual Most Popular Person in our graduating class?" I tease.

Clayton shakes his head, those long eyelashes catching the sunlight as he casts his gaze downward for a moment. "That was embarrassing," he says, "when that list came out."

Not as embarrassing as not being on it at all, I suspect, but I don't say that out loud. "You could always reinvent yourself at college," I tell him, thinking again of Dr. Paula and her three-pronged plan for self-actualization. "Be, like, Recycling Nerd instead of Soccer Dude."

"You know, most people don't realize this, but recycling is actually not the solution to any of our environmental problems whatsoever," Clayton says immediately. Then he smirks at himself. "Anyway, I don't know if it's going to be that easy. I've got this whole scholarship, you know? They're paying for Soccer Dude." He glances to his blind spot before pulling around a large tour bus emblazoned with a giant red maple leaf. We must be getting close. "How about you?" he asks in a voice that makes it pretty clear he wants to change the subject. "Northwestern in the fall, right? What happens after that?"

"Northwestern in the fall," I agree, surprised. Sure, I could basically have written an unauthorized biography of Clayton Carville for my senior research project. Still, it's strange to think he knows even this much about me. "Then law school. Internships with the Equal Justice Initiative or the Innocence Project. Sit for the bar. Clerkship. Practice for a while. Then, if I play my cards right, judgeship."

"Well, all right then," Clayton says, lips twitching. "Very decisive."

"I mean, yeah," I say, not sure if he's making fun of me or not. "I don't understand why more people aren't, honestly."

Clayton considers this for a moment. "What happens if something doesn't go according to plan?"

"Like what?"

"I don't know. Like if you don't pass the bar?"

I turn to look at him, alarmed. "Why would I not pass the bar?"

Now Clayton laughs for real. "I am sure you will pass the bar," he assures me. "But it does happen, you know."

I shake my head. "I've never failed at anything I've really tried to do." Of course, I tend to only attempt things I know I won't fail at, but that's neither here nor there. "I kind of don't believe in failure as a concept."

Clayton nods slowly. "You're kind of an intense person, huh?"

Right away my whole body warms, prickling and unpleasant. "I . . . have been told that in the past, yes," I admit, glancing down at my hands. I know I can be a lot sometimes, how hard I work and how badly I want things, how rigid my rules have always been. But it's like I don't totally understand how to dial it back before it—before my whole personality—tips into being Too Much. "Sorry."

"No no, it's not a bad thing," he amends quickly. "I'm just . . . observing."

Something about the way he says the word has me glancing over at him, curious. When I do, I find him gazing back at me, the same inscrutable expression on his face from the other night at the stoplight, in the instant before he looks back at the road.

"Anyway," I tell him, my skin heating up all over again, "you're one to talk. You're not exactly a failure yourself over there."

Clayton shrugs. "I've failed plenty of times," he says easily. "I play soccer, remember? I've lost more games than I've won. I don't think it's always a bad thing. Sometimes the failures are more important than the wins, you know?"

In my experience, this is emphatically something losers say in order to make themselves feel better; still, something about hearing it from Clayton makes me think about it a little differently. I worked so hard in high school to make sure that I would *never* fail. It's weird to hear someone like him talk about it as if it's actually a good thing.

"Huh," is all I say, reaching down into the grocery bag and pulling out a bag of Swedish Fish, ripping it open. Clayton holds out an open palm.

9

Clayton pulls off the highway in Mackinaw City, a town on the northern tip of Michigan. "I thought maybe we could take the ferry to Mackinac Island for lunch," he explains as we drive through town, turning into a parking lot near the water. "That sound okay to you?"

He literally could have suggested a meal of truck stop Funions and I would have been like, *Yep, sounds delicious,* but my smile now is wide and genuine. "That sounds awesome," I say truthfully. If this is a date—and I definitely, possibly think it might be a date?—it's 100 percent the best one I've ever been on.

It's also the only one I've ever been on, but still.

I grab my DiPasquale's hoodie off the floor of the SUV and trail Clayton across the parking lot, where we buy our ferry tickets from the kiosk. Clayton's phone dings twice with texts as he's paying for his, a frown passing over his face when he tugs it out of his pocket and glances at the screen. "Everything good?" I ask, his thumb flying as he keys in a hurried response.

Clayton nods briskly. "Yup," he says, shoving it back into his pocket without offering further explanation. "We're great."

Once we board, we head up top for a better view, settling ourselves into two seats near the edge of the boat as I tug my hoodie over my head, shivering in the chilly wind coming off the water. The ferry is bigger than it looks from the causeway, with a jet off the back that sprays a huge rooster tail of water as we tool along in the water. "That doesn't make it go any faster," Clayton tells me, gesturing with his chin. "It's just supposed to look cool."

"Hold on," I say, "should I add Ferry Captain to your list of aliases? Along with Soccer Dude and Recycling Nerd?"

"Frequent passenger," he corrects with a shake of his head. "We used to come up here every summer, that's all. My grandparents actually lived in Berlin, so we used to see them twice a year: every August here and every Christmas at their house."

I raise my eyebrows. "Berlin as in Germany?" I ask, and Clayton nods. "How's your German?"

He makes a face. "I mean . . . Oktoberfest?" he tries, and I laugh.

"Sure," I agree. "Also weinerschnitzel."

"Volkswagen," he counters.

"Kummerspeck," I remember suddenly.

Clayton shakes his head. "I'm sorry," he says, "what now?"

"It means 'grief bacon.'" It was a crossword clue not that long ago that stumped both me and Dad for the better part of the day.

"Literally, at least. But it's like, the food you eat when you're emotional."

"That's not real," Clayton says immediately.

"It's totally real!" I protest. "You can Google it!"

"Oh, I'm going to."

"You do that."

"I will."

"Okay, then."

We've turned to face each other now, my knees pressing against his on the bench seat; just for a second, Clayton's close enough to kiss. *What if I just did it?* I wonder suddenly. *What if I just leaned in, closed my eyes, and—*

Clayton clears his throat, straightening up again. "Kummerspeck," he mutters, shaking his head one more time.

※

Once we arrive on the island, I stake out a picnic table, posting up underneath a giant yellow umbrella while Clayton picks up food at a place called the Dog House. He's left his Tottenham hoodie—which I returned this morning, a little sheepishly—and his phone on the bench beside me, the phone basically glowing like a ten-thousand-point bonus prize in an old video game. I know it's wrong—that it's a gross violation of his privacy, that it crosses the line into actual creepy stalker territory—but I can't help but wonder about those texts he got earlier, and if they were from Bethany. Yeah, Clayton said they were broken up, but he also said things were complicated between them, which is basically the world's vaguest cop-out. I just need to understand what I'm dealing with, that's all. I just want to know what's going on.

I glance over at the line in front of the Dog House, making sure Clayton can't see me.

Then I pick up the phone and key in the first four digits of pi.

Sure enough, his most recent conversation is with Bethany: **I am beyond sad today,** she wrote as we were paying for our ferry tickets. **Can you come over? Bring green Pringles.**

I'm sorry kiddo, Clayton responded. **Can't today but I'll call you later. Are you okay?**

This whole thing just sucks, that's all. What are you doing?

"Hey," Clayton calls, headed back in my direction with an overflowing plastic tray. "Hope you're starving."

"It fell off the bench," I blurt out immediately, holding the phone up. My heart is pounding, both at the idea that he might have caught me and in confusion over what I just read. What "whole thing sucks" exactly? Bethany and Clayton's breakup? And why didn't he text back when she asked him where he was? If anything, I've got more questions now than I did before I snooped. "Sorry, I just . . . picked it up."

"Oh," Clayton says, apparently willing to take me at my word. "Thanks." He sets the tray on the table and tucks his phone back into his pocket. "Nothing but the finest," he jokes, handing me a hot dog and a bag of kettle chips, plus a black cow in a waxy paper cup. "Didn't know how you take your dogs, so I brought a little bit of everything."

"Mustard," I say absently. I'm super picky about my condiments. "Only mustard."

"You're going to have to learn how to appreciate Chicago-style next year," he warns me, doctoring his own hot dog with pickle relish, mustard, and ketchup. Then, once he's taken a giant bite: "You okay?"

"Oh," I say, realizing abruptly that I haven't touched any of the food in front of me. "Um, yeah." Nonna would probably say it serves me right to feel this way, that I got what I deserved for invading someone else's privacy. Dr. Paula would probably tell me to buck up and shine it on. And both of them would be right, theoretically, wouldn't they? After all, nothing has changed since twenty minutes ago. I still have no idea what's going on between Bethany and Clayton.

But Clayton is still here with me.

"So," I say brightly, reaching for my bag of kettle chips. "You guys used to come here every summer?"

He nods. "Usually my dad could only get away for a long weekend, but my mom and Ruthie and I used to stay for a couple weeks, sometimes even longer." Clayton shoos an obnoxious gull that keeps trying to hop up on the edge of our table.

"Does your dad work a lot?"

"Kind of. All those hips and knees that need replacing. And my mom is on like every board and committee imaginable, so. Neither of them are around a ton."

I think of my parents and Nonna, all of us perpetually on top of each other between the house and the restaurant, minding each other's business and breathing each other's air. It drives me up a tree sometimes, sure, but I also think I'd hate having it any other way. "That sucks."

Clayton shrugs. "It's fine. I mean, it was hard when I was younger. I just didn't understand why other kids' parents were always there and mine weren't." He makes a face. "Now I think it's, like, probably for the best."

I remember that night at DiPasquale's—the four Carvilles and their dour expressions, his parents' barely contained fight. "Are they . . . ?" I trail off. I'm trying to figure out how to put it delicately when suddenly something swoops down onto the table and in one quick movement, grabs the rest of my hot dog from its paper sheath. It smacks frantically against my face as it beats its retreat. I scream, more shocked than hurt, but Clayton jumps up, practically throwing himself on top of me and knocking me off the bench in the process.

For a moment I just lie there on the scruffy, rocky grass, Clayton sort of on top of me with a completely bewildered expression on his face. "What the heck was that?" he asks breathlessly, pushing himself partially upright. Our ankles are still tangled together, his bare skin touching the gap between the hem of my jeans and my sneakers.

"Seagull," I say, pointing behind us to where it flitted away. My

skin is tingling—the adrenaline rush from an avian near-death experience, sure, but that's definitely not all.

"Aggressive bastard." Clayton flops back against the grass beside
me, both of us laughing. "I thought it was like, an alien invasion."

While our food is left unprotected on the table, a few more gulls
start to approach. Clayton scrambles to his feet to try and chase
them off, but I shake my head. "Let 'em have it," I tell him, catching
him by the wrist. "You want to get out of here?"

"Let's do it," he says, taking my hand and pulling me to my feet.

✳

We hop onto the ferry, climb back into the car. "You sure you're
ready for this?" Clayton teases, keying the Canada Border Services
Agency into his GPS and pulling out of the parking lot. "Not going
to chicken out at the last second, are you?"

"I'm kind of worried it's going to be anticlimactic, to be completely honest with you," I confess, making a face.

"Oh yeah?" Clayton taps on the brakes, raises his eyebrows.
"You want to just forget about the whole thing and head back?"

I reach out and sock him in the arm, just lightly. "Don't you dare."

"Hey there, muscles," he says, grabbing my hand and squeezing,
holding on for a second before letting go. "No assaulting the driver."

We finally reach the border crossing, and the officer doesn't seem
at all surprised by our request. "So where are you from?" he asks,
looking from my passport photo to my face and back again.

"Michigan," I say.

"And how long are you staying in Canada?"

"Oh, about five more minutes," Clayton says cheerfully.

The officer nods, satisfied, the stamp hitting the blank page with a satisfying chunk. "Enjoy your visit," is all he says.

"Well?" Clayton asks once we're back out on the road. "You feel different?"

I look at him for a moment, the late-afternoon sunlight turning his skin warm and tawny. I can't believe he did this for me. Most of all I can't believe I let him.

"Yeah," I say, and I mean it. "I really do."

※

The ride home is mostly quiet—another episode of *[environ]Mental* and a little more Prime Country, Faith Hill crooning quietly as the sun sinks behind the trees to the west. "You want me to drive for a while?" I ask. Once we switch, Clayton falls asleep almost immediately, his head against the window and the vulnerable line of his throat exposed. It takes literally all my willpower not to reach across the center console and run one gentle finger along the skin there, just to see if it's as soft as it looks.

I don't, obviously. I'm not a total psycho.

But I think about it.

Eventually the gas light goes on, so I pull into a service station, Clayton blinking awake just as I put the SUV in park at the pump.

"Hi," he says with a yawn, the wet pink muscle of his tongue visible for the briefest of seconds. "Where are we?"

"Another hour from home maybe?"

He asks me if I want anything and runs into the mini-mart to pee, returning a minute later with a plastic shopping bag that he tosses into the back before climbing into the driver's seat.

"So," I say as we pull onto the highway—thinking again of his texts with Bethany from earlier, wanting to give him a chance to drop her into the conversation on his own. "What's your plan for the rest of the week?" By which I mean, *Are you planning to get back together with your maybe ex-girlfriend, and does "it's complicated" mean you guys still touch each other's bathing suit areas? Please advise.*

Clayton doesn't bite, though. Instead he tells me about the big soccer camp his sister is starting at Hope College in a few days, where he'll be helping with clinics. "There will literally be hundreds of kids from all over the state," he says, like he's not quite sure what he's signed himself up for. "It's going to be nuts."

I smile, trying valiantly—and utterly failing—not to be charmed by the idea of Clayton Carville teaching ten-year-olds soccer drills.

"What about you?" he asks.

This time, I tell him the truth. "Working, mostly. Hanging out with my grandma."

"She lives with you guys, right?"

I nod. "Nonna moved in when her husband died."

"Your grandpa?"

"Eh," I hedge, "not really. Bill was her fourth husband, and they were only married for a couple of years. I hardly knew him. They met at a Democratic Socialists meeting in Lansing." My actual grandpa died when my mom was a kid.

"Wait a second." Clayton's eyes widen. "Fourth?"

"Yeah," I say, laughing a little—in between Poppa and Bill were Silvio, who was very into model trains, and Victor, who had an extremely distracting mole on his forehead that I never quite managed to stop staring at. "She's Italian through and through in, like, the most passionate, stereotypical sense of the word. They call it *sanguigni*. She falls fast and hard. My mom was the same way."

"With your dad?"

"Um, yeah. But . . ." I debate telling him this next part. Not many people know that my dad isn't technically my dad, especially since he legally adopted me when I was in fourth grade, so we have the same last name now. It's not that I'm embarrassed about it or anything. It's just that I guess there aren't that many people I've ever been close enough to tell. "Before that, even. With my, uh, biological father."

Realization flashes across Clayton's eyes. "Oh."

"He was like, not that into the whole 'being a dad' thing," I explain, "so they broke up when I was still pretty small."

Clayton nods. "Do you remember him?"

I wave my hand, *so-so.* "It's not like my mom has a bunch of pictures of him for me to look at," I say wryly. "But sometimes I'll hear someone else say something in a certain way or with a particular cadence and I'll be like, 'Is that him?' " I crinkle my nose and change the subject. "Anyway, I'm like my nonna in a lot of ways, but that's not one of them."

"Oh no?" Clayton asks, glancing over at me in the passenger seat. It's fully dark by now, just the red glow of taillights up ahead of us and the fat white moon hanging low in the sky overhead. "So you don't have the . . . whatever you call it? Where you fall fast and hard?"

"*Sanguigni,*" I manage. "No, actually." I swallow hard. "I fall hard and then just kind of . . . stay there. Lying on the ground."

Clayton smiles out the windshield, just barely. "Good to know" is all he says.

We don't talk the rest of the ride, the air in the car getting heavier and denser between us, crackling with an electric energy that has every nerve ending in my body on high alert. It's like I can hear Clayton's heart beating. It's like I can feel the blood moving in his veins. By the time we turn onto my street, I half want to make an armpit farting noise or start singing "The Star-Spangled Banner" at the top of my lungs, just to break the tension.

But like, *is* it tension, even? Is Clayton feeling it too? Or am I having this extremely fraught experience completely solo, in the dank privacy of my own messed-up brain? I have basically no experience in this area whatsoever; the truth is that in all likelihood I've completely misread this situation and he's going to shake my hand at the end of the night like a freakin' job interview.

"I had fun today," he says finally, pulling up in front of my house and turning the car off. That's a good sign, right? It means he's planning to be here longer than it takes me to tuck and roll out of the passenger seat, at least.

"I did too," I tell him, tucking one leg up underneath me as I turn to face him. "Seriously, Clayton—this was really special, you doing this for me."

"Yeah, well." Clayton shrugs. "You're special." His expression turns immediately horrified. "Oh my God, that was so effing corny."

Holy crap. "No no, corny's okay," I say immediately, laughing nervously even as my heart slams against the inside of my rib cage like a furious zoo animal. "I love corny."

Clayton laughs, too, something like disbelief flickering behind his eyes. "Okay," he says. "Good."

"Good," I echo.

"Um, in that case," he says, shifting his broad body closer. "Can I, like—" He breaks off, blowing a breath out and swearing quietly. "Why am I nervous right now?"

"I don't know," I tell him honestly, though my own voice comes out slightly strangled. "I can . . . pretty much promise you there's no reason to be."

"Oh yeah?" He smiles at that and suddenly he's the same Clayton I've watched for years in the hallway—Soccer Dude, the most popular. The entire world, including me, at his feet. "So it's okay if I—"

"Yes," I say, then lean forward and kiss him.

Yes.

10

Up until this moment I have kissed exactly one other person—Charlie Patterson, who pecked me on the lips during a particularly mortifying round of Seven Minutes in Heaven at Ruoxi's birthday party in fifth grade. "Just get it over with," I told him, and he did, then spent the remaining six minutes and forty-five seconds showing me his Pokémon cards, which is not a euphemism.

Anyway. This is . . . not like that.

My damp palms land on his shoulders, Clayton cradling my head in one big hand as my body melts into his. His mouth searches mine, tentatively at first and then more firmly; I can feel his eyelashes brushing against my cheeks. The angle is kind of weird, honestly, both of us leaning across the center console and my spine twisting uncomfortably, but none of that matters because I am kissing Clayton Carville.

I. Am. Kissing. *Clayton. Carville.*

I keep waiting for my brain to quiet down, the whole universe narrowing to this moment like it always does for girls in books and fan fiction, but instead my mind is racing: *Am I doing this right? Is my breath okay? What's going to happen when we leave for college in six weeks?* In the back of my mind it occurs to me to wonder about condoms, which even through my haze of lust I recognize as a completely ridiculous thought. After all, it's not like I'm about to have sex with Clayton in his car on the street in front of my house.

But, like, *eventually* I might have sex with Clayton!

That is officially a thing that has entered the realm of possibility!

That's when my parents' front porch light flicks on.

"Oh, shoot," I say, pulling away dazedly, blinking. All at once it occurs to me that I never actually told anybody where I was going this morning. This could be sort of bad. "Okay. Um. I think I've got to go."

Clayton nods. "Okay," he says immediately, wiping the corner of his mouth with one thumb, then smiling a little. "I'll text you."

"Okay. Um. Bye!" I scramble out of the SUV, opening the door to the backseat to grab my DiPasquale's hoodie before slamming it shut again and booking it up the front walk. It's not until I'm digging my keys out of my purse that I even register the contents of the mini-mart bag that was sitting on the seat beside my sweatshirt—a tube of Sour Cream and Onion Pringles.

The green kind. The ones Bethany asked for.

I freeze for a moment, then whirl in the direction of the SUV just in time to watch its taillights disappear around the corner. *Come over,* she told him, like a spoiled queen summoning a courtier. But he can't possibly be headed . . . after we just . . .

Right?

I'm still standing on the steps trying to put a coherent thought together when my mom wrenches open the front door. "Where the *hell* have you been?" she demands.

I blink. She's never sworn at me in my life before, not ever. She looks terrible, her eyes red-rimmed and her dark hair a mess like she's been yanking at it. "I messed up," I say immediately, holding up both hands.

"Oh, I'll say." She opens the front door wider, taking me by the arm and tugging me roughly inside like I'm a toddler who nearly darted out into traffic. "Where were you?"

It occurs to me that Canada is probably not an answer that's going to win me any points at this moment. "I was with a friend," I tell her. Over her shoulder I can see my dad sitting at the cluttered kitchen table, looking equally wrecked. "This guy Clayton."

"Clayton?" My mom shakes her head, searching my face for clues. "Who's Clayton?"

"I know him from school," I tell her weakly. "I lost track of time, obviously, and—"

"You more than lost track of time, Rachel! It's almost midnight. None of us have heard from you all day. You didn't pick up your phone—"

"You didn't call me!" I protest, realizing even as the words come out of my mouth how extremely unlikely that is. I dig my phone out of my bag—where, I realize, it's been sitting on silent all day long while I was too distracted to check it. Thirty-seven missed calls, and just as many texts from my parents and Nonna. There's even one from Miles: **Yo,** he said, around four o'clock this afternoon, **just FYI, your parents are flipping the f out.**

I don't know what to say. I look to Dad for support, but he shakes his head. "Your mom's right. You were missing for almost an entire day. You're lucky we didn't call the police."

Holy crap. The *police*? "It wasn't like that," I try to explain, but my mom doesn't want to hear it.

"On top of everything else," she continues, "you just completely blew off work. No warning, no nothing. Poor Miles had to work the Cream Cart by himself—"

"I texted him, though," I defend myself. "He said—"

"Do *not*," she warns me, holding a finger up, and I snap my jaws shut. "We may be a family business, but this is a job like any other job. You scared the living daylights out of us—you scared the living daylights out of your seventy-year-old grandmother, I might add— and for what? To run around with some boy? I have never in my *life* known you to be so irresponsible."

The idea of Nonna worrying about me wrenches everything else into perspective; all at once, it feels dangerously like I might be about to burst into tears. I look at my dad, who stares down at his hands. "I'm really sorry," I say, my voice coming out small and piddly. "I have no excuse."

"No," my mom says flatly. "You don't." She takes a deep breath and lets it out slowly. "I cannot adequately communicate to you how relieved I am that you're all right, Rachel. But I also can't look at you right now. We'll talk about this tomorrow." With that, she walks out, leaving Dad and me alone in the kitchen.

Once she's gone, a thousand more excuses run through my head like a news crawl on a cable network: I'm moving out at the end of the summer. I'm almost eighteen years old. It was Clayton freaking Carville, king of Westfield High School; what else was I supposed to do?

Then I look at my dad, his shoulders slumped and his forehead wrinkled, and all the fight drains out of me for good.

"She's really pissed at me, huh," I say, flopping into the chair next to him.

My dad looks up, thoroughly uncharmed. "I'm pissed at you, too, honey." Then he sighs. "She's afraid of losing you, that's all."

"I'm sorry," I say again, reaching out and putting my hand on his. "But I was fine, really. It wasn't like—"

"No," he interrupts, "not tonight. Just . . . you've got a few more weeks and then, *poof,* you're gone. And that's a big transition for her."

"I mean, sure," I say, though the truth is I haven't actually thought that much about how my going away to college made my parents feel. "But it's a big transition for me too. And just because she's used to me living my entire life shut up in my room like a hermit doesn't mean—"

He holds up his hands to stop me. "I know it's big for you too.

And we're all going to have to do a little bit of adjusting. But try to remember you're steering this ship, will you? Your mom and I . . . we're just bystanders." He rubs his eyes again and shakes his head. "Try to cut us some slack, okay?"

I nod. "Okay."

"So," he says, leaning back in his chair and lacing his fingers together behind his head, looking at me speculatively. "Did you have fun, at least? With this Clayton?"

"Dad." I blush and glance down at my hands on the table, thinking about the entire day. The conversation. The boat ride.

The kiss.

I look up again, nodding a little. "You know what?" I tell him. "Yes."

✳

By the time I make it upstairs to my bedroom, I'm fully exhausted. I'm just climbing under the covers when my phone—which I've switched off silent, Mom—dings with a text from Carrie: **Um,** she wants to know. **Did you go to Canada today?** Then a moment later: **With Clayton?**

Holy crap, news travels fast when you're popular. **Who told you that?** I want to know.

I've got sources at the border, Carrie fires back immediately. **So what's up with you guys?**

He kissed me, I want to tell her. *He told me I was special.*

I think he also might have bought Pringles for another girl.

Oh, who knows, I type, trying my best to affect utter chillness. I take a deep breath. **What's up with him and Bethany, is probably a better question.**

Carrie doesn't answer for a moment, and I gnaw my thumbnail anxiously. She and Bethany have been best friends for a long time. **Sorry,** I type. **That was nosy.**

This time she writes back right away: **Nah,** she says, **you're fine. Nothing anymore, as far as I know. Why?**

Just curious.

Sure, sure. A winking emoji here. **Let's discuss this in person, yeah? Moxie's soon?**

I'm probably grounded until I'm forty. But after that, sure.

Sounds like a plan.

11

"Well, look who decided to grace us with her presence today," Miles says the following morning, which is predictable. He shoots me a cocky grin as he loads ladyfingers into the Cream Cart. "You know, I have to say, I'm kind of impressed."

I look at him dubiously, then double-check our sprinkle supply. "Meaning what, exactly?"

Miles shakes his head. "You of all people blew off a responsibility. Didn't know you had it in you. It's like you were channeling . . . me."

"Oh God," I say, truly horrified. "Anything but that." Then I frown, reaching back to scratch at my neck. "Sorry if I freaked you guys out yesterday, PS. I could have handled the whole thing better, probably."

Miles shrugs. "You're cool," he says easily. "Just glad you're not dead in a ditch with your hands and feet chopped off, et cetera."

"Aw, Miles." I bat my eyelashes at him. "You say the sweetest things."

By the time we get to the beach, there's already a small crowd waiting for us. Word of the ice cream Gondolas has traveled fast, and the cart sold out both days. Dad even got extra gelato delivered with the hope that we can start filling up twice a day on weekends.

"So," Miles says, his voice muffled as he leans over the cooler, scoop in hand. "What did you get up to yesterday, anyway?"

I press my lips together, trying not to smile too hard at the memory. "I left the country, actually." It sounds so absurd that if my cheeks weren't still wind-burned from that boat ride, I might doubt it actually happened at all.

Miles straightens up, looking over at me in surprise. "What?"

"I mean, just to Canada." I zip an Amex through the card reader before passing it back across the counter. "But still."

"That's random," he says, dropping the Gondola into its waxed paper sleeve and thrusting it wordlessly at our waiting customer. "You realize people usually commit a crime first. Did you commit a crime first?"

"Have a good day!" I call pointedly, then look back at Miles. "No, I did not commit a crime first. I didn't have any stamps in my passport, that's all. Clayton took me across the border so I could get one." It sounds a little like I'm bragging, which I guess makes sense since I kind of am.

Miles, however, looks unimpressed. "Oh" is all he says.

I frown. "What?"

"Nothing," Miles says. "So, are you going to have, like, a million of his babies now or whatever?"

"What?" I feel myself blush. "No. I don't know. Jeez."

"Okay." Miles busies himself wiping the counter.

"What?"

"Nothing!"

"Miles, I swear to God—"

"Just—" Miles looks over at me, shrugging a little. "Be careful with that dude, okay?"

I frown, thinking of the text messages and the Pringles can and the "It's complicated." "Why?" I ask, trying to sound casual. "What do you know?"

"I don't know anything," Miles says stubbornly.

"Well, that's a fact. But—"

"Can you not be a pain in the ass for one second?" he interrupts, sounding wounded. "I'm trying to help you here." He sighs, scrubbing his hands through his dark, messy hair. "You know my house is across the street from Bethany's, right?"

"Yes," I say, already not liking where this is going. "So?"

"So, Clayton's car is over there. Like, a lot."

"Oh," I say, feeling relief course through me. "Yeah, no, I know. But they broke up."

Miles looks skeptical. "They broke up since last night?"

That stops me. "His car was there last night?"

"That giant SUV with the youth soccer sticker on it?" he asks. "Yeah." Then, off what I'm assuming is my stricken expression, he sighs. "Look, I'm not trying to shit stir."

"Aren't you?" I snap.

"No, actually," Miles fires back. "But if it were me, I would want somebody to tell me that my new boy toy's car was in his old gal pal's driveway all night last night." His eyes widen meaningfully. "Like, until this morning."

"I . . . Oh." I feel my whole body deflate, my stomach suddenly queasy as if I'd eaten our entire supply of Gondolas in one gluttonous sitting. "Okay." Yeah, Clayton told me things were complicated between him and Bethany. Yeah, I saw those chips in the back of his car last night. But I didn't actually think they were still—

He made me feel like—

What kind of person—

"Rachel," Miles says, and his voice is so quiet. He takes a cautious step in my direction, and for one deranged second I think he's going to hug me, but in the end all he does is nudge me gently out of the way so he can get to the counter.

"Hey there," he says brightly, greeting the next person in line like he's the king of customer service. "What can I get you?"

※

I spend the rest of the afternoon in a deep, malignant sulk, the cloud above my head dark as a midsummer thunderstorm. Miles tries to cheer me up by making off-color comments about unsuspecting passersby, but it's no use, and we work the last hour of the day in dreary silence. "Look on the bright side," he instructs as we part ways back at the restaurant. "Sooner or later, he definitely would have given you chlamydia." I flip him the bird in reply.

Back at home, I shovel a couple slices of reject pizza into my face—buffalo chicken and jalapeno, so spicy it makes my nose run—before shuffling upstairs and flopping face-first onto the mattress. I'm scrolling through Snapchat for the millionth time today, looking for further concrete evidence of Clayton's betrayal, when my phone dings with a text from Soccer Dude himself.

Hey, he says. **You around tonight? There's a 7:15 Indiana Jones at the dollar theater that a bunch of people are going to.**

Like Bethany? I think snottily, throwing the phone across the mattress before leaning over and picking it up again. **Can't,** I tell him. **Grounded.** I don't actually know if this is true—my mom hasn't said a word to me all day beyond "wear sunscreen" as Miles and I set out with the Cream Cart this morning—but it sounds plausible, at least.

Shit, Clayton says. **Because of yesterday?**

Yep.

A pause here, then: **You okay?**

Fine.

Are you sure?

I bite my lip. **Yup,** I text.

Another pause and I think he's going to push me—let's be real, I *hope* he's going to push me; that's why I'm being such a pill to begin with—but in the end he just sends a thumbs-up emoji. **Okay. Have a good night.**

So, I think, collapsing back onto the pillows and staring up at the ceiling. *That's that, I guess. Good try, Dr. Paula! Sorry my young life is already too pathetic for successful course-correction!*

Then I sit up again, so fast it almost makes me dizzy. No, I decide. That's *not* that. After all, why should Clayton get off that easy while I sit at home and brood? He kissed me. He took me to freakin' Canada! At the very least, I deserve closure.

I cross the room and dig through my closet, feeling a momentary pang of annoyance at Past Rachel for choosing a wardrobe that, for the most part, did not spark joy, before pulling on jeans and a V-neck T-shirt and heading downstairs. My parents are closing at the restaurant tonight, which means they won't be home for another couple hours, and while I'm pretty sure the fact that they haven't explicitly grounded me yet isn't cart blanche to do whatever I please, what they don't know won't hurt them.

The dollar theater is one of my favorite places in town, actually—this old-fashioned movie house that was restored a few years ago by an eccentric rich guy with fond memories of watching black and white movies there back when he was a kid. It's got plush red seats and a cool art deco marquee and shows mostly tourist-friendly modern classics, stuff like *Toy Story* and *Troop Beverly Hills,* plus the occasional weird experimental film.

Clayton and his friends are buying their tickets at the window when I approach, the smell of buttered popcorn drifting out the front door and hanging like a scrim in the warm, humid air. "Hey," he says when he sees me, offering me a surprised smile. "Your parents change their minds?"

I don't smile back. "Not exactly," I tell him. "Can I talk to you for a second?"

Clayton glances from me to his friends, then back again. Bethany isn't here tonight, I notice, but Tricia Whitman is watching us curiously. Spencer doesn't bother to hide his smirk. "Uh, sure" is all Clayton says.

He follows me around the corner to the side of the theater, where posters covered in Plexiglas announce baby-friendly matinees and a midnight showing of *The Princess Bride.* "I just came to tell you I don't think we should see each other anymore," I announce.

Clayton blinks at me for a moment. He's wearing frayed green shorts and his Tottenham hoodie, a pair of Wayfarers hooked in the neck of his T-shirt. He looks so deliciously summery; it makes me want to punch him in the throat.

"Okay . . . ," he says slowly, shaking his head a little. "So you came out to tell me we shouldn't . . . go out?"

"Yes," I say imperiously, not liking how ridiculous he makes it sound. "Listen, yesterday was fun. But next year you're going to be in Milwaukee and I'll be in Chicago—"

"Evanston," he corrects.

"Whatever. Same difference."

"I mean, sure," Clayton says, tucking his hands into his pockets.

A furrow has appeared between his eyebrows, cautious. "But I guess I just don't see what that has to do with, like, right now? I thought we had fun yesterday."

Oh, that infuriates me. "Is *that* what you want?" I demand, ignoring a startled look from a mom passing by us with a pair of little boys in tow. "Somebody to have fun with on the side and then throw out at the end of the summer?"

"What? No, of course not, but—" Clayton frowns. "I don't know what I want, Rachel. I thought we were getting to know each other, figuring it out." He shakes his head one more time. "And what do you mean, on the side?"

"I know about you and Bethany."

It's my trump card, my smoking gun, but Clayton just stares at me blankly. "You know *what* about me and Bethany?"

I open my mouth, then close it again, caught up weirdly short. "Well, I know you stayed at her house last night, first of all."

"You—" Clayton's features twist unpleasantly. "Did you *follow* me?"

"Of course not!" I snap, offended, although I guess I can't totally blame him for jumping to that conclusion. He did catch me spying on them from my bedroom window the night of the party. And— even if he doesn't know it—I did creep on his texts. "A friend of mine saw your car."

"Okay. Well." He doesn't even bother to try and deny it. "Look," he says instead, "I already told you, things are complica—"

"How *complicated* could they possibly be?" I interrupt. "Either you guys are together or you're not, and if you're not, then I don't see why you need to be at her house in the middle of the night—"

"And I don't see how that's any of your business!"

"It's my business because you made me fall for you!"

"I made you—" Clayton throws his hands up. "We went on *one date*!"

Well. That stings.

I clamp my mouth shut, pressing my lips together even as my eyes start to prickle. It's not even the words that hurt, exactly—of course it was only one date; of course I know that. It's the way he says it. Like I'm completely delusional. Like I'm some inexperienced little kid with a crush.

And maybe I am.

I knew I had no business trying to do this. I knew I had no business trying to be anyone else.

"Okay," I say finally, hanging on to my composure with claws and teeth. I clear my throat, square my shoulders. "Well. It was fun. Thanks again for the passport stamp."

Clayton blows a breath out. "Rachel," he says, and his voice is gentler now, "don't—"

"Bye, Clayton," I tell him firmly. Then I turn around and go home.

12

To my surprise, the grounding I'm fully expecting never arrives. Instead, my mom decides I should *work off my debt to the society of this family* by spending my day off from DiPasquale's washing the windows at the house.

All of them.

Inside and out.

It's hard, tedious work—we don't have the fancy windows that release with the flick of a lever, which means there's an awful lot of yanking involved—and I spend the better part of the morning climbing up and down the ladder, my back and biceps singing. "Can you please be careful?" I yell down at Jackson, who's supposed to be holding the ladder steady. "If I fall and break my neck, it's on you."

"It's fine," Jackson says, though even from my vantage point I can tell he's only got one hand on the damn thing, using the other to scroll through his phone.

"Jackson!"

It's late afternoon by the time I'm finally finished and head upstairs for a shower. I'm sweaty, I'm smelly, and I have a big red scratch on my forearm from the particularly finicky pane on my parents' bedroom window.

But at least it distracted me from thinking about Clayton.

He hasn't texted since last night, not that I was expecting him to. Still, I kind of hoped. I know I was an idiot for trusting him, for thinking I was the type of girl he actually wanted to be with. For thinking he was the type of guy *I* wanted to be with.

I was wrong, that's all, I tell myself firmly as I climb out of the shower, wrapping my hair in a towel and padding down the hall to my room. And in a few weeks I'll be at Northwestern and none of this will matter.

My real life can get started. Just like I've always planned.

Miles texts as I'm wriggling into a pair of leggings. **Wyd?** he wants to know. **Still crying into your cornflakes over Mr. Popular?**

I roll my eyes. The truth is, I'm miserable. I wish I could rewind the last forty-eight hours entirely, even if it meant missing out on the trip over the border, and go back to admiring Clayton from afar without ever speaking to him, just like the universe obviously intended. Every time I close my eyes, I hear his incredulous voice—*we went on one date*—and can barely resist the urge to fling myself into Lake Michigan.

But I'm not about to tell any of that to Miles.

Did you need something? I ask. **Or did you just want to heckle me?**

Mostly just want to heckle you, he writes back immediately. **But also just saw there's new episodes of that corny feminist superhero thing you like on Netflix, if you wanted to come by and watch.**

Huh.

I sit down hard on the edge of my mattress, my damp hair dripping onto the pillows. I was just talking about that show in the kitchen at the restaurant the other day, but I'm surprised he was even listening, let alone that he voluntarily wants to put it in his eyeballs. **It's not corny. It's amazing,** I tell him, though the truth is it's actually kind of both. **Tonight?**

Unless you were planning to spend the evening wailing and rending your garments.

I roll my eyes, full intending to tell him to go screw . . . but then I think about it. Hanging out with Miles has actually been kind of fun lately—working in the Cream Cart, taking that hike—on top of which it's not like I've got anything better to do tonight. Before I can quell the impulse, I find myself imagining Dr. Paula with a big bowl of popcorn in her lap, watching as our heroine takes down the most insidious supervillain of all—the patriarchy.

Okay, I decide, hitting SEND before I can think better of it. **Can I bring anything?**

Wait, Miles writes back, **you're actually coming?**

What the hell? I have just about had it with stupid boys and their mixed signals this week. **You just invited me, didn't you?**

No, I did, he says immediately. **And I meant it. I just didn't think you'd actually say yes.**

Yeah, well. I pull a tank top over my head, trying not to think about the fact that I've been sitting here for the last ten minutes texting him in just my polka-dot bra. **I'm full of surprises.**

You know what, though? Miles asks me. **It turns out you kind of are.**

✳

"It *is* you!" Miles's mom crows when she flings open the door to their house a half hour later, her voice familiar as the *Sesame Street* theme song, which she used to sing with us when we were small. "When Mi said you were coming over, I thought he was kidding."

"It's really me," I say. Miles and I see each other all the time because of school and work, but we don't exactly hang out, and it's been a while since I've seen his parents. His mom—who I've always known as Julie, except I think it's super weird to call adults by their first names, so mostly I don't call her anything at all if I can help it—is a few years older than mine, the kind of person who gets all her clothes at Ann Taylor and never goes too long between haircuts. If she and my mom hadn't grown up together, I don't think they'd actually have anything in common—not, I think suddenly, unlike Miles and me.

"The house looks amazing," I tell her now, looking around at the airy foyer. Last time I was here, the clean white walls were covered in a dated ivy-print wallpaper, with heavy curtains framing the windows. Now the whole place looks fresh and bright.

"My God, that's right," Julie says, her smile falling a little bit as she follows my gaze. "You probably haven't seen it since—"

"Yeah." Tommy's memorial service. I can't help but think back to that day, even though I know we'd both rather forget it: the four identical Edible Arrangements lined up like sad soldiers on the counter, a late-summer rain turning the front yard to mud. Miles's parents hadn't been expecting to host a gathering, so half the house was under construction, the dining room basically taken down to the studs. The whole thing was a mess in more ways than one. "Um, my mom said you guys did the kitchen too?"

"We did!" Julie tells me, brightening again as she puts an arm around my shoulders. "Come on, I'll show you."

Before I know it, I know more than I ever wanted to about Carrara marble and silent-close drawers and "dentil molding," which sounds like something you need Novocain for. Julie's fixing me a cup of Earl Grey tea when Miles traipses in.

"When did you get here?" he asks, looking at me with something akin to suspicion. His hair is damp, and he smells faintly of Dial. I can't help but wonder if he showered specifically because I was coming.

"Hello to you too," I say pointedly. "A few minutes ago."

"I stole her away," Julie tells him, handing me the mug and

squeezing my shoulder. "It was great to see you, honey. Tell your mom I'll call her this week."

"Sorry about her," Miles says once she's gone, getting himself a can of pop from the enormous refrigerator. He's wearing jeans and a different T-shirt than usual, the word *Rogue* emblazoned over the NASA logo. His bare feet are long and pale.

"No, it's fine," I say, shaking my head. "It was good to see her." I hold up the grocery bag slung over my arm, setting it down on the expansive island. "I brought snacks."

"Nice," says Miles. Then, as he peers at its contents: "Holy shit, you brought *throwback* snacks."

"Yeah, kind of." I went a little crazy at the store on the way over, picking up cheddar Goldfish and Fruit by the Foot and two-tone string cheese, all the stuff we used to eat when we were small. "I feel like adult life doesn't offer enough opportunities to eat Go-Gurt."

"Hey, speak for yourself," Miles says, but his smile is more genuine than I'm used to seeing it. "This is awesome. Come on, let's go downstairs."

Miles and Tommy used the basement as a playroom when we were kids, and I'm expecting the high school version of that: dated sofas and dingy lighting coated in a layer of Cheetos dust, that old-sock teenage boy fug. But it turns out that this space has gotten the same Chip and Jojo makeover as the rest of the house: an oversized sectional with a full canoe and oars hanging on the wall behind it, a foosball table, and a wall of built-in bookshelves. There isn't a TV, although some kind of high-tech projector hangs close to the ceiling: "That wall has special paint that turns it into a high-definition screen," Miles says.

"Seriously?" I step closer to examine. It looks like all the other walls, but with the press of a button, the projector sets it alight. The glow of the menu is partially blocked by my shadow. "That is so cool."

"Welcome to the future, Walls." Miles grins.

"Thank you," I say dryly, looking around for another moment. The far wall is covered in a series of black and white photos, artfully displayed gallery-style. The Vandenbergs at Disney, Miles and Tommy each wearing matching Pluto baseball caps. Miles and his mom at our middle school graduation. Miles and Tommy building a snowman, bundled up in parkas and snowsuits until they're barely recognizable. Even I make an appearance, I notice with a start: There's a shot of me and Miles running through the backyard at twilight, our pudgy toddler hands just barely touching, my sundress tangled around my knees.

"So when did this all get redone?" I ask, grateful that Miles is fussing with one of the eighteen remotes and didn't see me staring at the photo. "The basement, I mean."

Miles shrugs. "Couple years ago?" he guesses, flopping down onto the sectional. "After Tommy died, my mom went into a sort of HGTV tailspin. She went from a room-by-room plan to the whole damn house right-this-very-minute." He shrugs. "Honestly, I'm surprised my dad didn't erect a life-size bronze statue of him down here."

I open my mouth to say something but think better of it, sitting down a few cushions over from him on the sectional and slipping off my flip-flops before tucking my bare feet underneath me. "Good to have projects, I guess."

"I guess so." Miles glances at me sidelong. "I mean, don't get me wrong, I'm not complaining. I'm probably going to be living down here until I'm forty, so, like, I appreciate the amenities."

"Oh, get over yourself." I toss a Fruit by the Foot in his direction. "You are not. You could probably get a coding job in like two seconds, if you wanted one."

Miles tears open the foil wrapper, cuts off a six-inch strip. "I actually already have an offer," he confesses, sticking it into his mouth.

"Seriously?" I whip my head around to look at him. "Where at?"

"Some health insurance company out of Detroit," he says once he's swallowed. "It's not exciting or anything, but it pays. My mom wants me to do a couple years of at least community college first, though."

I raise my eyebrows. "What do you want?"

Miles shrugs. "Honestly?"

Part of me is surprised he's even offering the truth as an option. "Honestly," I echo.

"I was kind of hoping maybe I'd get recruited."

I grin at him; I can't help it. "Like, by the NFL?"

"Funny girl." Miles makes a face. "No. Have you ever heard of white hats?"

I shake my head.

"It's a kind of hacker that, like, sneaks into companies' networks to find flaws," he explains. "With their permission, obviously. Nothing nefarious."

"That's a job?" I ask, leaning back against one of the four dozen color-coordinated throw pillows. "I mean, there's actual money in it?"

"Tons," Miles says, finishing the rest of his fruit snack and reaching for the bag of Goldfish. "Well, technically there's more in real hacking, but that carries with it the pesky threat of prison time." He shrugs. "Radware hosts a big competition every year. I'm saving up to go next summer. It's somewhere different every year, all over the world. Chile, Germany, France." His whole demeanor shifts as he talks about it, I notice; he isn't even trying to mask the enthusiasm in his voice.

"Wow," I say once he's finished. The last time I heard him talk so excitedly about something was probably his WWII phase in second grade. "That's cool, Miles. I had no idea you had, like . . . goals."

"Yes, thank you," he says, rolling his eyes a little. "Hopes and dreams, even."

"Well," I say. "Color me shocked."

I'm teasing, but for once Miles doesn't play along. "I swear," he says, dumping a handful of Goldfish into his mouth, "sometimes it's like everybody thinks all I do is make sandwiches and play video games."

"Hey," I say, shaking my head a little. I think of what he said a minute ago, about the bronze statue of his brother, then reach out with one foot and kick him gently in the thigh. "That's not what I think."

Miles looks at me with some interest. "Oh no?" he asks, and it sounds like a challenge. He reaches down and grabs hold of my ankle. "Then what do you think?"

That stops me, every nerve ending in my body on alert in half a second; his grip on my ankle is warm and surprisingly strong. "What, like, about you?"

"Yeah." His gaze is steady.

"I . . . I don't know," I say, flustered. All of a sudden it's like the rules of this conversation—the rules of our entire *relationship*—have completely changed. "I have no idea." I glance around the room, my gaze finally lighting on Tommy's vintage Star Wars figurines, displayed in a Plexiglas case. They're 1977 Kenner originals. I know because Jackson used to beg to play with them and Miles wouldn't let him. "You still have those?" I ask.

Miles makes a snorting noise, low and animal. I'm 100 percent sure he's about to make fun of me, but in the end he just lets go of my ankle like nothing happened. "Yep," he says, and he is so, so casual, "but Barkley ate Obi-Wan a year or two ago. So that's the only one missing." He shakes his head. "Hopefully someday I'll track down a replacement."

He picks up the remote again, dims the lights, and clicks over to Netflix. "Okay," he says, nodding at the projector wall. "You want to watch this dumb thing or what?"

"It's not dumb," I insist, my voice coming out the slightest bit whiny. For one truly ridiculous second I consider kicking him again, just to see what he'd do.

The show starts, but it's difficult to concentrate for several reasons: one, it *is* a little dumb, even though I do think good feminist representation is important.

And two, I can tell Miles isn't paying attention either.

Neither one of us acknowledges it—the way we're both edging a tiny bit closer together on the sofa, how every so often I catch him glancing at me out of the corner of his eye. The skin of my ankle pulses hotly where he touched it, like a branding iron.

I'm busying myself dissecting a string cheese into the smallest possible particles when Miles puts one arm behind his head and slouches down against the pillows, his shirt hiking up just slightly. It's the same thing that happened when he was under the Cream Cart the other day, except now I'm suddenly extremely aware that we're alone in his darkened basement; in the glow of the screen I can see the sliver of skin that's revealed, right where his jeans sit low on his hips.

Celestial girdle, eleven letters, two words. Starts with *A*.

Apollo's belt.

Oh my God. What is *wrong* with me? Two nights ago I was making out with Clayton Carville in the front seat of his SUV, and now . . . I shove the rest of the string cheese into my mouth, washing it down with a gulp of cold Earl Grey.

"What happened there?" Miles asks as I'm setting my mug back on the coffee table.

"Huh?" I blink at him. It's the first thing either of us has said in an episode and a half. "What?"

"On your arm." He reaches out and runs one blunt fingertip along the scratch I got from my parents' window this afternoon, so gentle it's almost like he isn't touching me at all.

I look from his finger and up at his mouth without entirely meaning to. Down at his finger again. "Oh." My voice comes out shaky and breathless. "Um. Window washing accident."

Miles looks at me for another second, biting at the corner of his lip before nodding. "Watch your stupid show" is all he says.

13

I meet Carrie at Moxie's for ice cream a couple nights later, the two of us waiting for the better part of half an hour on a line that snakes clear down the boardwalk. Moxie's is a landmark in town, an old-fashioned sundae shop with fake Tiffany lamps hung over every table and walls festooned with all kinds of vintage memorabilia: old metal signs and yards of fishing net, a full-size rowboat suspended from the ceiling. There's even a working wooden phone booth tucked into one corner, which I used to love to shut myself inside when I was a kid. Now it's practically a rite of passage for couples at school to take pictures of themselves kissing inside it, which is called being *#MoxiesOfficial.*

Not that I would know.

Tonight the leather booths are packed with families stuffing themselves with banana splits and ice cream sundaes shaped like clowns. I count at least three Scooper Bowls, which each contain a full gallon of ice cream and are free if you can manage to consume them in one sitting. Carrie and I bail out once we've gotten our milkshakes, weaving through the crowd and heading down the boardwalk until we find an empty bench that faces the water.

A thing I always loved about Carrie when we were kids was how easy it was to be around her, and tonight I listen gamely as she chats about the wacko tourists who wander into the gallery all summer looking for souvenirs—"Souvenirs!" she says, sounding offended. "Like they think we're going to be selling seashell art and those airbrushed T-shirts that say, like, *Surf's up!"*—and her dads' newest rescue cat, Salvador Dalí. He brings the total feline population in her household to three, Carrie tells me, all of whom are named after famous artists of the Dadaist movement. "I'm kind of worried about what's going to happen when I move out," she confesses.

"Worried how?" I ask, taking a sip of my shake. "Like you're going to come home at Christmas and it's going to be like the Old Woman Who Lived in a Shoe and all her children?"

"Exactly." Carrie nods. "Except my parents are an interracial gay couple and the children are cats." She makes a face, stretching her long legs out in front of her. "So," she says, her voice just the slightest bit sly, "speaking of nothing at all except that I'm curious, how's your summer of new experiences treating you?"

I huff out a laugh. "I don't know," I say. I think of Clayton, who's disappeared from my life just as quick and definitively as he turned up in it. I think of Miles's gentle fingertips skimming over the broken skin on my arm. "Confusing."

Carrie raises her eyebrows. "In a sexy way?"

"In an embarrassing way, more like."

"Well." Carrie shrugs. "That's just the price you pay for being a person out in the world, right?"

"For me, maybe."

"For everyone," she counters immediately.

I shake my head, dismissive. "Not you."

"Seriously?" Carrie asks, looking askance in my direction. "You think it makes you special because you've embarrassed yourself in front of a hot guy or two? I literally tripped over nothing in front of Adam the other night and went sprawling face-first down the stairs at his parents' house."

"What?" I laugh for real now; I can't help it. "You did not. Are you okay?"

"Oh, I did," she assures me, her full lips twisting. "I'm fine. Only hurt my pride, blah blah."

"What happened then?"

"We laughed it off," Carrie says with a shrug, flashing me a grin. "And then we made out for a while."

"I mean, well played." I hold my milkshake up in a salute.

"Thank you."

We're quiet for a moment, facing the water, listening to the rhythmic pound of it against the shore. "I don't know," I say finally. "It just seems like it's so much easier for other people, you know? Being a . . . what did you call it? A person out in the world. For somebody like . . . Bethany, for example. It just feels like she knows how to do it."

I try to make it sound like I'm just coming up with Bethany's name as a random example and not like she's my chief romantic rival in the tragic opera I have been composing in my head the last few days, but Carrie's not buying. "Uh-huh," she says dryly. "That's because your entire concept of Bethany as a person is based on you, like, stalking her Instagram or whatever."

I blow a breath out, insulted. God, does *everyone* think I'm a huge creep? "Who says I stalk her Instagram?"

"I do," Carrie deadpans, "because I know you."

"Fine," I admit sulkily.

"Bethany's life isn't perfect," Carrie says. "She's got her shit, just like everybody else. Somebody stuck a maxipad to her back during senior week. Didn't you see that?"

"What?" My eyes widen in horror. "No!"

"Of course you didn't," Carrie says, sounding pleased with herself. "Because she didn't put it on social media."

Truthfully this anecdote satisfies me in a small, mean way, because apparently I am a giant monster, but I take Carrie's point. It's not just experiences I missed out on all these years by refusing to put myself out there. It's people too. The versions of them I've had in my head all this time—of Bethany, of Clayton, even of Miles—are mostly just stories I've made up to tell myself, to keep me from being too lonely.

"Can I ask you something?" I say, scraping my nail along the ridges ringing the lid of my waxy paper cup. "As long as we're talking about Bethany?"

"They're broken up," Carrie says in a voice that communicates pretty clearly she's told me that already.

"Okay, but like . . . are you sure?" I explain about Miles seeing Clayton's car in her driveway the other night, leaving out the most humiliating parts of our argument in front of the dollar theater. "It probably doesn't make a difference at this point. But I just want to know."

"Hmm." Carrie nibbles her straw thoughtfully. "I mean, to be completely honest with you, if they're back together, I might not be the first person she talked to about it."

"Really?" That surprises me. "I thought you guys were, like, best friends." I make a face. "Saw it on her Snapchat and everything."

"Cute," Carrie says. "I don't know, things have been kind of weird with us lately."

"Weird how?"

"I don't know," she says again. "It's not like we had a falling out or anything. We're just . . . not as close as we used to be, all of a sudden."

"That sucks," I tell her honestly. "It's hard to grow apart from somebody like that."

"Yeah." Carrie glances at me sidelong. "It is."

I take a deep breath. "Look," I blurt out, because one of us has to bring it up sooner or later, and maybe one of the things I'm saying yes to this summer is being a person who brings up hard topics. "I'm really glad we've been hanging out lately. And we definitely don't have to talk about this if it's going to ruin it or make it weird. But like, did we do something, way back when? Me and Ruoxi? To make you not want to hang out with us anymore?"

"Wait." Carrie's dark eyes narrow. "What?"

"I'm not mad about it," I promise her. "It was a long time ago, clearly. I just always wondered."

Carrie looks at me like I've totally lost it. "You think *I'm* the one who ditched *you guys*?"

I frown. "Yes?"

"Rachel, you guys didn't want anything to do with me."

"What?" Now it's my turn to gape. "That is fully untrue."

"It is true!" she says, sounding surprisingly hurt after all this time. "You guys were girl geniuses—which is obviously fine and great, and the last thing I'm going to do is begrudge you your freakin' brainpower. But it was like eventually you just got bored of me or something."

"Huh? No!" I shake my head. "That's not what happened."

"Um, yeah it is," she says with a nod. "Remember that summer program at Hope College in sixth grade? Or the debate team? Or the quiz bowl tournaments in seventh grade?"

"Yes," I say slowly, not sure what that has to do with anything. "Of course."

"Well, I don't," Carrie says flatly. "Because you guys didn't invite me."

"I—" Oh.

I think back on the end of middle school, realizing with a warm rush of shame that Carrie has a point: It *was* me and Ruoxi, a lot of the time. The two of us sitting in the back of her family's minivan on our way to the quiz bowl in Grand Rapids. The two of us staying up too late in the dorm room at Hope College's summer program. My dad picking me up from Ruoxi's after a late night of practicing for debate team. "I didn't . . . I mean, you never said anything."

"What was I supposed to say?" she asks. " 'Hey, guys, don't leave me out just because you think I'm a moron'?"

"You're not a moron," I say immediately.

"I know I'm not a moron!" Carrie laughs. "I'm just not, forgive me, a giant school nerd." Then she smiles. "But that doesn't mean I didn't want to be around you guys. Or, more to the point, for you guys to want me around."

"We *did* want you around," I tell her. "We used to spend all this time trying to figure out why you didn't like us anymore. Ruoxi had this whole giant conspiracy theory going. But then when you started being friends with Bethany and Tricia, it was like, oh, obviously the answer is that we weren't cool or popular enough for you."

"It wasn't like that," she promises. "And they're not that cool or popular, for the record. They're just normal, when you actually get to know them."

"That is fully a thing that only cool and popular people say," I counter.

Carrie smirks. "Maybe. I don't know. It doesn't matter now, does it? I mean, we're all going off in a million directions and it doesn't matter who was like what in high school. We can all just kind of like . . . be who we actually are."

I think of what Clayton said the other day, about how he was still going to have to be Soccer Dude even once he left for college. "I hope so," I tell her. "That sounds really nice."

We're quiet for another minute. I finish my milkshake, setting my cup down on the boardwalk at my feet. "For the record," Carrie says quietly, "I'm really glad we're hanging out now too."

I swallow hard, my chest tight. "I'm really sorry we left you out," I tell her. "And for all the dumb time we lost."

"Yeah," she says. "Me too." She clears her throat then, like possibly I'm not the only one feeling a little bit emotional. It's hard, being a person in the world.

"So hey," she says as we head back along the boardwalk, "what are you doing Friday? Adam's having a party, if you want to come by."

I shake my head. "I already checked 'party' off the list, remember? I feel like that means I should be exempt for the rest of the summer."

Carrie snorts. "I'm *pretty* sure that's not how it works. Come on," she urges. "It'll be fun. And he doesn't even have a pool, so you're totally safe there."

"Maybe," I promise as we part ways at the edge of the boardwalk. "We'll see."

"I don't know, Rachel." Carrie shakes her head, braids swinging. "Sounds like a yes to me!"

14

*T*he following day is freezing—by July standards anyway—and except for a couple people out running, the beach is empty. "You realize the Venn diagram of the types of people who run in this weather and the types of people who want to impulse-buy ice cream sandwiches are two completely separate circles," Miles announces, peering up at the ominous-looking rain clouds. "Should we just pack it up?"

I grimace. "And go do inventory with everybody else back at the restaurant?"

"Fair point." Still, it's not like Miles is wrong: the Cream Cart's customer base is basically entirely contingent on the weather, which despite my control-freak tendencies remains infuriatingly out of my realm of influence. We haven't sold a single Gondola all day. "Can we go somewhere else, maybe? Down by the arcade?"

"Too close to Moxie's," I point out. "But I wonder if there's like a festival or a camp or something that we could—" I break off. *A camp,* I think, flushed with pleasure at my own quiet brilliance. That's it. And if it happens to be a camp where I might or might not run into Clayton Carville and he gets an eyeful of how fabulously I am doing without him, well, that would just be an added side benefit, wouldn't it.

I grin across the Cream Cart at Miles, flipping the storage compartments shut with a satisfying chorus of clicks. "Let's go to Holland."

"What, for the tulip festival?" Miles raises an eyebrow. "You know, you stick one toe over the Canadian border and now all of a sudden—"

"Hope College," I interrupt, impatient to get going. "There's a soccer clinic there this week—and if we leave now, we can probably catch people right as they're picking up their cranky little athletes."

Miles eyes me for a moment, an expression on his face like possibly he can see the tissue underneath my skin. "A soccer clinic, huh?"

"Yup," I say primly, daring him to make a comment. "Is that a problem?"

He shakes his head. "Sounds great," he says, digging the keys to the cargo truck out of his back pocket. "Let's go."

※

Turns out we've timed it perfectly, staking out a tree-lined corner of the college parking lot just as the clinic wraps up for the day.

We've barely gotten set up before we're completely mobbed by a throng of sweaty, hungry kids and their parents; in fact, we're so swamped we stop taking custom orders and Miles makes up his own combos. "Chef's choice today, mate," he says, handing one to an eager-looking ten-year-old. It feels like this is where the entire tween population of Michigan is hanging out today.

No sign of Clayton, I can't help but notice. I can't decide if I'm disappointed about that or not.

"Holy shit," Miles says once the rush has dissipated. "Was that seriously less than an hour?" He nods his angular chin at my apron pocket, which is bulging with a fat wad of cash. "Is that money in your pocket or are you just glad to—"

"Do not," I cut him off, using a plastic spoon to flick some left-over Stracciatella in his direction. It lands on his nose and he doesn't even blink.

"What's wrong?" he asks with a laugh, reaching up to wipe it off. "Do I have something on my face?" I watch the way he bites the pad of his thumb, feeling my cheeks warm.

Oh my God. What is with me lately that I keep having this reaction to him? Am I actually, like, physically attracted to Miles?

Holy crap, do I like Miles?

I don't have time to dwell on it, because—predictably—the next thing he does is grab a spoon and return the favor, flinging a blob of Gianduja at me. His aim isn't as good as mine, though, and it lands right on the collar of my DiPasquale's T-shirt, dripping down into my shirt.

"Nice," I say, rolling my eyes at him before reaching for a paper napkin. "Thank you."

"You're welcome," he says pleasantly. "You missed some." Then, without waiting for me to take care of it, he reaches out and swipes his thumb right over my collarbone, dipping ever so briefly into the neck of my shirt.

It's a lot, the sticky coldness of the ice cream and the slight pressure of his fingers on the side of my throat, and I gasp without entirely meaning to. It's not a bad gasp, strictly speaking—it's not, if I am being totally honest, a gasp that means I don't like what you're doing right now—but still Miles backs up right away.

"Sorry," he says. "Not trying to cop a feel."

"Oh no?" I manage, coming back to myself enough to tease him. "If you were trying to cop a feel, I'd know it, et cetera?"

"Exactly." Miles coughs, turning back to the empty cooler; even from this angle I can see that his ears have gone pink. He's embarrassed, I realize suddenly. Miles Vandenberg, the crown prince of the double entendre, the person from whom I first heard an *are you just happy to see me* joke to begin with, is embarrassed. It kind of makes me feel like I'm the valedictorian all over again.

"Okay, weirdo," I tease, dumbly fond of him suddenly with his stupid messy hair and crooked tooth and thick eyebrows, the scar on the side of his chin from where Tommy beaned him with a remote control when he was five. "I see how it is."

Miles makes a face at me over his shoulder. "Oh," he says,

seeming to finally register that I don't in fact feel anything close to harassed at this particular moment, "I'm the weirdo."

"You are always the weirdo, yes."

"I will keep that in mind."

"You do that."

"I will."

Miles shakes his head, smiling a little. We work in silence for another couple of minutes, wiping down the counters before loading the cart into the back of the cargo truck. "So," I say as we climb up into the cab, "what are you up to tonight?" The truth is, I don't want this day to end yet.

"Ugh, screw me." Miles rolls his eyes and groans, banging his head lightly against the seat. "I had actually forgotten until right this second, so thank you for that. I've got this thing I have to do."

"Mysterious," I tease.

"It's . . . truly not." He shakes his head. "It's for my mom. It's 'Dine Around' tonight."

"Dine Around?" I repeat.

"Yeah," Miles says. "It's this thing for the Historical Society—"

"Yeah, no, I know what it is," I say, unable to keep the smirk off my face. At least, I have a vague idea: a bunch of middle-aged women paying a bunch of money to go snoop around other peoples' houses while they eat appetizers and drink Dixie cups of white wine. "Nonna did it one year, but she said you didn't get enough booze for your buck."

"Nonna is correct," Miles tells me flatly. "But my mom got really into it after my brother died, and she's the chair this year, so I told her I'd help her out a little."

"That was sweet of you."

"Yeah, well, I'm a sweetheart."

"Uh-huh. What do you have to do, stand around serving baby quiches for three hours?"

"Worse."

"What?"

Miles closes his eyes, shaking his head like it's too gruesome even to contemplate. Then he opens one again. "Actually," he says, looking at me speculatively. "You wanna come see for yourself?"

15

"*You* know," I tell Miles a couple hours later, "when you said you were helping your mom out a little, this is not exactly what I pictured." The two of us are standing on opposite sides of a partitioned storage room at the Historical Society, changing into musty-smelling period costumes. I think I'm meant to be some kind of flapper, in a fringy black dress and a feathered headband. I can only imagine what Miles is dressed as.

"You were really hoping for those baby quiches, huh?"

"I mean, yes," I admit, my stomach rumbling; neither of us has eaten anything since we loaded up the Cream Cart this morning. "But also I figured we'd just be standing on a corner somewhere handing out maps or helping clueless tourists not go into the wrong house."

Miles cackles. "Can you imagine someone wandering into Mrs. Sheffield's garden and expecting to be not only welcomed but also supplied with libations?"

"Mrs. Sheffield probably spends Dine Around evenings on her porch with an actual shotgun on her lap, daring anyone to try and trespass."

"That's how she spends all her evenings," Miles fires back. "You ready?"

"I guess so?" I put the headband on, then grab my real clothes and stash them in my bag before stepping out around the partition.

Miles looks at me speculatively and I'm expecting some kind of raunchy comment, but all he does is nod. "Not bad."

"Thanks." He's wearing a '20s-style fedora with a fat black band around it and a button-up shirt and regular pants. "No fair. How come you get to look normal?"

"Right," he says, raising his arm to reveal a gangster-style holster. "Never leave home unless I'm packing heat."

I tilt my head to the side like, *Fair point.* "Remind me again what we're doing, exactly?"

"I told you," he says patiently. "We're hosting."

"Hosting *what*, though?"

There's a knock on the door and Miles's mom pokes her head in. "Capone, you ready?" Then, beaming at me: "Oh, Rachel, you look like a regular Daisy Buchanan."

My gaze flicks from Julie to the fedora and back again. "Capone?"

"Didn't Miles tell you?" she asks. "This year's theme is Roaring Twenties. There are three sites here in town, and then Felt Mansion is the final stop for everyone. Jazz in the gardens, cocktails, a special

presentation. I have to say, this is an extremely well-chaired event."
She winks at Miles and he groans playfully.

"Capone and his goons used to stay at the hotel in town and the
Felt Mansion," Miles explains, gesturing down at the suit and holster. "Thus the getup. Though I'm way better looking, obviously."

"Obviously," his mom and I chorus dutifully.

"All right," Julie says, reaching out to straighten Miles's tie. "You
two need to get up to Felt by five-thirty, okay? Ask for Donna and
she'll tell you where to go and what to do. The buses and guests
arrive at six, so you all better scoot." She claps her hands. "And
have fun!"

✳

"Oh good!" Donna says when we arrive in the lobby of the mansion, checking something off on a flower-patterned clipboard. She's
a heavyset woman in her fifties in an expensive-looking suit the
color of ripe eggplant, an expression on her face like this is not her
first Dine Around rodeo. "Here's our star of the evening. Now, you
know your lines?"

Star of the evening? Lines? I whirl around to look at him.

"Ready to go," Miles assures her, assiduously avoiding my gaze.

I fully intend to give him boatloads of shit about this newest
development, but all at once Donna is taking my arm and leading
us over to the far end of the lobby, where a handful of other flapper

girls and dudes dressed similarly to me and Miles are leaning against the wall. "You all will be handing out these information brochures about supporting the History Center or if you're of age, helping the catering staff with beverage trays."

"Not a baby quiche in sight," Miles murmurs mournfully. "You sure you don't want to back out now?"

"Are you kidding?" I whisper back. "You have *lines*."

"Miles?" Donna asks, interrupting us. "I need you. Now."

Miles's eyes widen playfully. "She needs me," he echoes, reaching out and chucking me on the chin, old-timey gangster style. "Be good, doll."

I roll my eyes and grab a stack of the brochures from the table. It reminds me of the brochures the Canadian immigration officer handed Clayton and me, and for a second a pang in my chest threatens to settle in. I tamp it back down, standing there with the two other flapper girls who don't seem like total prima donnas as we wait for the Dine Around guests to arrive. I catch a glimpse of Miles across the room as he listens to whatever instructions Donna is gravely imparting, nodding at her with great tolerance, even affection. I can't believe he's voluntarily subjecting himself to something like this.

I can't believe he's letting me *witness* it.

Once the first bus turns up and the guests are milling around, the jazz trio starts playing. I spy Miles across the patio, leaning against a wall scowling, and I'm about to wander over to him and see what his problem is when it occurs to me this is him in character. All at once, I completely understand why his mom not-so-gently suggested he do this. It's so . . . him. He catches me staring and shakes his head, covering his mouth with his hand to hide his smile.

Just then, Donna's voice echoes over the speaker: "Ladies and gentlemen, it is my honor to welcome you tonight to the Felt Mansion." She's standing on a small stage, dressed now as a flapper in a gown way fancier than the rest of ours. She's also wearing a metric ton of makeup that wasn't there before. "As you know, the Felt Mansion was finished in 1928, built by self-made millionaire Dorr Felt and his wife, Agnes, who—"

"Yeah, yeah, yeah. Quit yer yakking," Miles's voice comes over the speaker. Donna looks flustered and I wonder if he cut her off early before realizing that of *course* he did.

He's Miles.

I smile as I watch him saunter forth, clambering onto the stage and nudging her aside. He starts talking about his gang of bootleggers who spent a lot of time in this "neck of the woods." "We sure do enjoy the hospitality. The weather. And, of course, the ladies." He wiggles his eyebrows and steals a glance at me.

I'm totally losing it by now, and I almost miss the rest of his monologue, which is mostly just more about the community in the '20s and what a roaring good time they had. "Now, please, enjoy yourselves this evening. And might I recommend the Gin Fizz? It's delicious."

Miles comes over after accepting a few compliments from

fawning older ladies dressed from head to toe in Lilly Pulitzer. "That was . . . quite the performance."

"Thank you." He grins. "When Mom told me I'd get to be Scarface, I kinda thought there'd be more fake tommy guns involved. Some bathtub gin at least." He lifts the glass of Coke somebody's handed him, wipes at the black streak on his cheek. "At least the scar part is fake."

"Seriously, though." I shake my head, with that same feeling I had when he told me he was in therapy—like possibly there's a whole other side of him I'm only just waking up to, that he's only just started trusting me enough to let me see. "That was cool of you, doing that for your mom."

"Yeah, yeah." Miles waves me off, nodding at a cater waiter strolling by with a silver tray hoisted on one shoulder. "Baby quiches, mothereffer," he crows triumphantly. "Let's go."

※

I hang around the Felt Mansion with Miles for another hour or so, picking at the appetizer trays as surreptitiously as possible and hiding a smile as a steady stream of women my mom's age wander over to flirt with him. "Who knew you were so popular with the over-forty set?" I tease as we head back out to the parking lot.

"I mean, I knew," Miles fires back, digging his car keys out of his pocket. "Cougars love me."

"Don't say cougar," I chide automatically, settling into the passenger seat. Miles drives a low-key black Civic that used to be Tommy's, a mostly-peeled-off Iron & Wine sticker still adhered to the front of the glove compartment. Miles would probably die of embarrassment if anyone ever thought he listened to Iron & Wine.

"What's wrong with cougar?"

"It's gross."

"You're gross."

"Oh, very mature."

Miles grumbles good-naturedly, rolling the windows down as he pulls out of the parking lot. It's a warm, humid night, the brackish lake smell of home just barely perceptible on the air. It occurs to me all at once how much I'm going to miss that smell when I leave in a few weeks. "You need to get home?" he asks.

I glance at the clock on the dashboard. "I've got some time, actually." I told my parents about Dine Around when we dropped by the restaurant to return the Cream Cart after our shift this afternoon, and apparently a Historical Society benefit synthesized closely enough with my usual nerdy extracurriculars that neither of them questioned it or even told me what time to be home. "You hungry?"

Miles glances over at me, looking surprised. "Sure."

We head over to the Shak, a divey burger place not far from the boardwalk, still dressed in our flapper finest. The Shak used to be "Shake's," but over the years the sign out front lost the apostrophe and then the *E* and the *S* and no one ever bothered to replace them.

Miles pulls the greasy front door open, and I duck under his arm to step inside.

At the counter, he insists on ordering in character as Scarface, all "two Number Ones and a pop for the lady, nice and quick so nobody gets hurt." I roll my eyes at him, charmed in spite of myself, even as the cashier looks like he's never been so unamused by anyone in his entire life.

"You realize he's probably spitting in your food right now," I tell Miles quietly as we settle ourselves at a two-top by the window. "And my food, most likely."

"Extra protein," Miles says, no hesitation at all. He's himself again now, tie loose around his neck and the sleeves of Capone's dress shirt rolled up to reveal the sharp knots of bone in his wrists.

"Where did you learn how to do all that?" I ask, taking a sip of my Coke. "And when?"

"What, like, pretend to be a 1920s gangster?" Miles shrugs. "I don't know. Movies, I guess. And I did that kids' theater thing when we were in elementary school."

"Oh yeah." I remember that, vaguely, Mom and I going to see him in *Seussical* at the community college. We brought him a bouquet of grocery-store carnations. "You ever think about getting back into it?"

"Acting? No." Miles shakes his head. "I don't know. I do enough of it in everyday life, probably."

I tilt my head, intrigued. "Deflecting?" I ask pointedly.

Miles makes a face. "I'm sorry I ever told you that, I swear."

"No, you're not."

Miles's eyebrows quirk. "No," he agrees after a moment, "I guess I'm not."

"What do you think would happen if you stopped?" I ask. "Deflecting, I mean."

I'm expecting a snotty answer, but Miles actually seems to consider it, sitting there quietly in his wobbly burger joint chair. "Honestly, Rachel," he says finally, curling both hands around the edge of the chipped melamine table, "I think that possibly the world would eat me alive."

I blink, my heart doing something weird and twisty and unfamiliar deep inside my chest. "Miles," I start to say, but the guy brings our burgers just then and we inhale them in not-uncompanionable silence, passing the ketchup and Shak sauce back and forth across the table. I want to tell him . . . something, but I can't decide exactly what.

Once we're finished, we head back out to the parking lot, neon lights from the boardwalk blinking in the distance. "We should probably drop these back at the Historical Society," Miles points out, motioning to our costumes. "You know, now that they smell like fryer grease and human desperation."

"Okay. Yeah." The truth is I'm hardly listening. I stop short when we get to the Civic, leaning back against the trunk and turning to face him, shifting my weight in my uncomfortable borrowed flapper shoes.

"Listen," I announce before I can talk myself out of it. "For the record. If you were honest with more people about who you are and how you feel—if you stopped deflecting so much, or whatever—I don't think the world would eat you alive."

Miles raises one eyebrow, takes a step closer. He does smell like fryer grease, actually, but also like himself. "Oh no?" he asks, tucking his hands into his pockets.

"No," I tell him, squaring my shoulders. "I think you're smart and occasionally funny and actually sort of decent, when you want to be. And I think the world, like, responds to that kind of thing. Positively."

Miles's lips twist. "Occasionally funny," he mutters, shaking his head. "Thanks."

"Can you shut up for a second?" I complain. "I'm trying to tell you something nice about yourself and you're too busy being a dope to even register it."

Miles looks at me then—really looks at me, full on, in a way that makes me suddenly very aware that my back is pressed up against the trunk of the Civic. "I'm registering it," he says quietly, taking another half step closer. "I promise."

"Are you?"

"Yeah."

I swallow. "Okay, then."

"Okay, then," Miles echoes. "Can I say something now?"

I sigh theatrically. "If you must."

"I—" He breaks off, shakes his head. "I don't actually have

anything," he admits, and I'm starting to make an irritated sound but then he puts both hands on my face and kisses me.

He's a better kisser than Clayton, is my first thought, which is fully shocking because (a) I would have bet a considerable amount of money until this moment that Clayton has kissed significantly more girls than Miles, so either I'm wrong and Miles is a secret ladies' man or he's just, like, naturally extremely talented at kissing, and (b) how am I suddenly in a position to be comparing the makeout techniques of two different guys when literally one week ago the entire breadth of my life experience was Charlie Patterson and his Pokémon cards? I should send Paula Prescott a fruit basket, assuming she's still alive.

But not now.

Like. Definitely not now.

Right now I am busy.

Miles keeps one hand on my face and rests the other on my rib cage, nudging my mouth open and sucking gently on my lower lip. My own hands are just kind of hanging there like two dead birds until finally my crude motor skills come back online and I reach up, wrapping my arms around his neck so we're pressed together from chest to thigh.

"Rachel," Miles mutters, his smile slow and sly against my mouth. I can tell from the tone in his voice that he's going to make some dumb joke that's going to break this moment and make it absolutely necessary to talk about this: what it is or what we're doing, what any of it might mean. It's exactly the kind of thing I'd want to talk about, normally, the kind of conversation I'd force with anyone else, but here in this parking lot with the person I've known longest, I look in his eyes and shake my head.

"Not yet," I tell him firmly, then pop up on my tiptoes and kiss him again.

16

A few days later, I'm covering a front-of-house shift at Di-Pasquale's so one of the new girls can take her food safety class. I hand a pair of women their laminated order number and tell them their food will be right out, then grab a tub of dirty dishes out of the wait station and bring them back to the kitchen. Miles, who's hard at work on a chicken parm Gondola, catches my eye and winks.

I stick my tongue out and head back to the floor even as a full-body flush works its way up from my toes. I can't stop thinking about our kiss the other night. More than that, I can't stop thinking about the fact that we've kissed twice more since then: the following afternoon behind the garlicky plastic curtain in the wait station while Michael Bolton piped in over the speakers, and then again in the cab of the truck before we returned the Cream Cart yesterday, only breaking apart when Miles accidentally leaned on the horn.

It's Miles. It's *Miles.*

And I am feeling . . .

Something.

"Excuse me?" someone says, startling me out of my thoughts. When I look up from the counter, I find Bethany Lewis blinking back at me. She's dressed in a pair of immaculate white shorts and the kind of perfectly fitted T-shirt that probably cost as much as my parents' car, her hair waterfalling over her shoulders in perfect waves. "Hi," she says, smiling a smile I usually associate with middle-aged white women asking to speak to my manager. "It's Rachel, right?"

I barely resist the urge to roll my eyes, my innate panic at the sight of her giving way to annoyance. Why is she pretending she doesn't know who I am? We've gone to school together since we were, like, six. Is it some sort of psychological trick? Is she here to make a scene about Clayton? Is she here to challenge me to a duel?

Okay, now I'm back to panic again.

I nod. "Can I help you?" I ask, sliding a menu across the counter in her direction. She glances at it momentarily, then shakes her head.

"Actually, I was hoping to talk to you for a minute."

"To me?" Bethany and I have literally never had a conversation in all the years we've not-known each other, and the last thing I want to do is start now. "Um, sorry. I'm . . . working?" I glance around the mostly empty restaurant, which definitely does not require my tending at this particular moment. "Kind of a busy time."

Now it's Bethany's turn to be irritated, her glossy mouth turning down at the corners. "Look," she says, "it'll take two seconds, okay?"

I hesitate. I may be shiny-new Rachel these days, thanks to Dr. Paula, what with my cascading party invitations and many suitors, but at the end of the day she's *Bethany Lewis*. And old habits die hard.

Deferential in manner. Eight letters. Ends with *T.*

Obeisant.

"Sure," I hear myself say, untying my apron and following her over to a booth in the corner—the same one she was sitting in with Clayton the day I spilled the Italian soda all over him, which feels like a whole lot longer ago than just a couple of weeks. I wonder if she thinks of it as her booth; I wonder if she thinks of Clayton as her Clayton, and I'm so busy wondering that I don't notice until after we sit down that Bethany Lewis . . . doesn't actually look that good today.

It's a mean thought to have, the kind of girl-on-girl negativity they'd frown on in my feminist superhero show, but it's also kind of true: There are dark circles under her eyes that even her fancy concealer can't hide. Her hair doesn't seem as shiny as usual. And her expensive T-shirt has a tiny smear of toothpaste on the neck.

It's the toothpaste that gets me most, actually, and I feel myself softening. "So," I say, trying not to sound like a total snotrag, "what's up?"

Bethany blows a breath out. "Look," she says again, "first of all, Clayton doesn't know I'm here."

My stomach turns over unpleasantly. So this *is* about Clayton, then. Not that there was anything else it could reasonably have been about, I suppose, but I guess maybe there was a tiny part of me that was hoping she wanted to be my new best friend or at the very least wanted me to participate in her multilevel marketing scheme. "Okay," I manage, finding a rogue straw wrapper on the table and twisting it around my fingers.

"Second of all, he and I are not together. At all."

My head snaps up. "You're not?"

Bethany ignores me. "Third of all," she continues, not bothering to hide her incredulity at this juncture, "he likes you. Like, a *lot*. And he told me you basically lost your mind about him staying over at my house the other night—"

"I didn't *lose my mind*," I defend myself, humiliated. Holy crap, is that what he's telling people? "We went on one date."

"Okay, well, whatever." Bethany is unmoved. "He said you were very upset and that you guys haven't talked since then, and like—" She breaks off now, her composure slipping for the briefest of moments. "Clay's been a really, really good friend to me lately. And I don't want to mess things up for him just because my life happens to be a disaster and he's been trying to help me."

"Okay," I say slowly. It's only now that the reality of what Bethany's telling me is starting to sink in. *Clayton likes you. Like, a lot.* Holy crap, it's better than being valedictorian all over again; it's like that plus a full ride to Northwestern and a brand-new car all rolled into one. Still, I think again of our fight outside the movie theater, humiliation flaring inside me like a torch. "I don't get it, though. If he likes me so much, then why wouldn't he just explain—"

"Things are complicated," Bethany interrupts, impatient. "But that doesn't mean—"

"Can I tell you something?" I blurt out. "I'm so sick of people telling me things are complicated. Like, I'm pretty smart. I don't see why he couldn't just be honest about what he was doing over there and trust me to—"

"I mean, some things are just not your business, Rachel!" Bethany sits back hard against the vinyl bench and throws her hands up, the gesture surprisingly violent for such a pristine individual. "Like, what do you want to hear? That my dad's been cheating on my mom for eleven years and has a whole other family in Minnesota and we all just found out and so sometimes Clayton comes over to bring me junk food and watch movies and keep me from totally losing the plot? Does that make you feel better about yourself? Like, congratulations, my life is not perfect, whatever you might think."

I blink, stunned into silence. Bethany is breathing hard. She looks like she wants to rip my lungs out, and also she looks completely horrified. I can tell she didn't mean to say any of that at *all*, and that's how I know it must be the truth.

"I'm sorry," I say, which is of course massively inadequate. I'm a smart person, sure. But I have no idea what I'd do if something that *complicated* ripped through my family like a hurricane, pulling up trees and knocking whole houses down. "That's awful."

"Yeah, well." She yanks a napkin out of the dispenser and uses it to carefully wipe underneath her eyes, like she knows instinctively her makeup has migrated. "It's not great. But that doesn't mean I want my dad to ruin Clayton's life on top of everyone else's just because he can't keep it in his pants." She grimaces. "My dad, I mean. Not Clay."

"I get it." I'm silent for a moment, that weird post-adrenaline exhaustion coursing through me, when all at once I have a thought. "Does Carrie know?" I can't help asking. "About your dad?"

Bethany looks at me a little oddly, shaking her head. "No," she says. "Nobody does, except Clay." She makes a face. "And now you, I guess. Which, like, I would really appreciate it if you didn't tell anyone, okay? It's not exactly the kind of thing I'm advertising all over the internet."

"No, no," I say quickly. "Of course not." I think of what Carrie said that night on the boardwalk, about how my entire concept of Bethany was based on what I'd put together from social media, from the carefully curated stories she chose to tell to the world. Suddenly so many things make sense: Bethany and Clayton shut up together at Spencer's party. The can of green Pringles. The chasm Carrie felt growing between them, even if she wasn't sure exactly why.

"You should tell her, though," I say. "I mean, not if you aren't comfortable. But she knows something is up, and she misses you." I shrug. "I can tell."

"Yeah." Bethany tilts her head back, peering up at the drop-in ceiling for a moment. "I should tell a lot of people probably. But

I keep putting it off. And now it's turned into this big secret I'm keeping, and everybody is going to be, like . . ." She waves her hand vaguely.

I don't know her well enough to interpret the gesture, whether she means mad or judgy or something else altogether. "I mean, I obviously have no idea what it's like to be in your position," I tell her. "But most of your friends don't either. And so they have no right to fault you for choosing to deal with . . . this . . . however you felt like you could."

Bethany raises her neatly sculpted eyebrows. "You think?"

I nod.

"Thanks." She smiles weakly as she slides out of the booth to leave. "Well, I'll let you get back to work," she says. "This was . . . weird. But I'm glad we talked."

"Yeah," I tell her, and I'm surprised to find that I mean it. "Me too."

Miles comes out of the kitchen as the bells on the door jingle behind her, his eyes the size of two large pizzas. "Was that Bethany Lewis?" he asks, incredulous. "What did she want?"

I look from him to the door to the crumpled-up napkin Bethany left on the table for me to deal with, feeling more confused than I ever have.

"It's complicated," is all I say.

※

After work I plunk myself down on the front stoop of my parents' house and text Clayton. **I think I owe you an apology,** I type.

I'm half expecting him to ignore me, but he texts back right away: **You think? Or you know?**

My heart stumbles at the sight of his words on the screen, sure as if he were here and said them out loud. **I know. Bethany came and talked to me at the restaurant today.**

Ah.

Yeah. I gnaw my thumbnail. **Anyway. I know I came on a little strong that night outside the movies. You must think I'm a total basket case.**

Clayton shoots me the thinking emoji, hand on his skeptical yellow chin. **I mean, not a TOTAL basket case.**

I huff out loud, even though there's no one to hear me. **Mean!**

I'm joking, he promises quickly. **And I know I probably came off like a giant sketchball with all that "it's complicated" shit. It just wasn't my secret to tell.**

I get it, I tell him honestly. **I think . . . high school was just a really different place for me than it was for you. Does that make sense? So when you started hanging around and seemed interested or whatever, I was just waiting for the other shoe to drop. And then when I heard you spent the night at her house, it just felt like . . .**

Boom?

I let a breath out. **Exactly.** If I'm being honest with myself, it was almost a relief to think he'd messed up so quickly. I'd spent so long imagining Clayton as this perfect human specimen that I was sure there was no way he could possibly measure up in real life. And sure, some of that was a healthy skepticism, a way of protecting myself, but the truth is there was a part of me that wanted to believe the worst of him, because it proved I hadn't been wrong to close myself off for so long. And how messed up is that? Wanting someone—wanting the *world*—to be a disaster, just for the sake of being able to feel secure in missing out.

Well, he says now. **I am interested, or whatever. So what do you think? Can we start over?**

Um.

I gaze out at the quiet evening, the whole neighborhood settling down for the night: a sprinkler arcing lazily back and forth across the street, Jamie Oliver the corgi lounging on the porch next door.

Can we start over?

I can't help but think of Miles just then, with his Al Capone swagger and his surprising, disarming sweetness. I would have bet good money that I'd had the full Miles Vandenberg experience way before this summer's little experiment, that he was one person I knew inside and out. But it turns out I was wrong about that too. Do I really want to give that up before it's even really started?

Still, this is *Clayton* we're talking about, who I've wanted for longer than I can even remember.

Clayton, who suddenly wants me too.

I don't want to stop seeing Miles.

And I also don't want to say no to Clayton.

Could I just say yes . . . to both of them?

I mean, it's crazy. But then I think about Dr. Paula and *The Season of Yes*. I think about all the boys—or, okay, the *potential* for boys—I said no to over the years. And now . . .

Wasn't this the whole point of this summer—to say yes to new experiences? To say yes to things I really want?

You know, I type slowly—stretching my legs out in front of me, breathing in the sweet summer air. **I think we probably can.**

17

*T*he following day is, by all accounts, perfect beach weather. The water is calm and the sort of deep, rich blue that makes you forget that the body of water you're looking at is in fact a lake and not an ocean; except for a few poufy white clouds, the sky is clear and bright. I've never been much of a surf and sand kind of girl—just one more thing I've reflexively figured I wouldn't like, I guess—but working the Cream Cart with Miles, perspiration trickling down my back inside my DiPasquale's T-shirt, I find myself rethinking my stance.

It's been a busy—but kind of annoying—shift so far, a stream of tourists who don't quite get what we're selling and the credit card machine needing to be rebooted every other transaction. I can feel Miles losing his patience, wound like a spring about to snap. "What can I get you?" he asks now, wiping the sheen of sweat from his cheekbone with his forearm as a small girl and her dad approach the cart.

The little girl hems and haws, changing her mind three times before demanding a SpongeBob Popsicle, which we emphatically do not carry. Miles cracks his neck left, then right, then left again. He doesn't roll his eyes exactly, but it's a near thing.

The girl finally makes her decision and her dad forks over four dollars, telling me to keep the change with a tone of great generosity that belies the fact that Gondolas cost $3.75. "Gee, thanks, mister," Miles says as he presents the girl with her gelato, adding a bit of flourish and a wide smile that's primarily for my benefit. "A whole quarter."

The dad shoots us a nasty look before ushering his daughter away across the boardwalk. "Can you cool it possibly?" I ask Miles once they're gone. "Like, yes, they were a couple of jerks, but there's no reason for you to be one too."

Miles frowns, unabashed. "Why?" he asks, reaching for his water bottle. God, it is hot out here. "I'm never going to see those people again. What's the point?"

"Seriously?" I ask, feeling my temper flare as I count off on my fingers. "One, because you're actively wearing a shirt with the name of my parents' livelihood on it. Two, because the social contract is literally what makes civilization work, even if you think it's stupid. And three, because you weren't raised in a barn."

Miles's eyes widen. "Jeez," he says, looking wounded. "Sorry."

I exhale noisily, holding my hand out for the water bottle. I can't help wondering if I'm feeling less patient with him than usual on account of Clayton suddenly popping back into the picture. The thought makes me feel about two inches tall. "Sorry," I say, bumping Miles's shoulder with mine. "I'm wound a little tight this morning, clearly."

"Uh-huh," he says, making a big show of looking me up and down. "Wonder what we could do to fix that, possibly?"

"Down, boy," I chide, even as a tiny thrill rumbles through me. I nod across the boardwalk, where two little kids are approaching the cart. "All right. Let's practice."

Miles raises an eyebrow. "Practice what, exactly?"

"Your customer service skills, perv." I gesture to the beach that's brimming with tourists. "I know you can do it. And who knows?" I reach down and slide a finger through his belt loop, yanking once. "If you're successful, maybe you'll get a reward."

He does better this time, chatting with the boys about which flavor combos are best, even smiling as they hand their money over and again as they take their first massive bites. "See?" I tease, poking him in the ribs. "You're a natural."

"Oh, right." Miles grabs my finger and squeezes, making a face that suggests he hasn't forgotten about the aforementioned reward. "So here's a question," he says, leaning back against the cooler and crossing his ankles. "You have plans tomorrow night? You want to do something?"

He's just one click too casual for it to be genuine. I tilt my head, tickled. "What, like a date?"

Miles sighs. "Yes, princess. Like a date." He raises his eyebrows. "You interested?"

I am, in fact, and I'm about to tell him so when a thought occurs to me. "I do have plans, actually," I say, which is both the truth and extremely surprising to realize. Dr. Paula would be proud. "I said I'd go to a party with Carrie. But you could come, if you want?"

Right away, Miles shakes his head. "I don't know if you've noticed this at any point in our, oh, eighteen years of acquaintance, but I'm not really the partying type."

"Neither was I, until this summer," I point out. "Come on, it could be fun."

Miles snorts. "Listen to you," he says, still shaking his head a little.

I can't tell if he's finding me charming or not. Other people trying to convince me to do supposedly fun things used to drive me up a tree, pre–Dr. Paula. It feels a little unfair to turn around and do the same thing to Miles, like possibly I'm changing the rules on him.

But also, I realize with a little bit of a shock: I want to go to that party.

"I'll consider it," he says finally, taking a step closer. I can smell his deodorant working, the warm sheen of salt on his skin.

"You do that," I fire back.

I'm about to tilt my face up and deliver on that reward when my phone buzzes in my back shorts pocket. I fish it out and peer at the screen, tilting it away when I realize the text is from Clayton. **Hey you,** he says. **Want to hang out tonight?**

Oh boy.

I glance around and look at Miles, who's turned to help some customers. I bite my lip. **Sure,** I type, my thumb moving almost of its own volition. **Sounds great.**

18

I text Clayton to see if I'm going to need my passport again, but it turns out we're just headed to the same boardwalk where I've spent the better part of this summer working the Cream Cart. "Sorry if this is like, super boring," he says as we stroll past Moxie's, looking a little embarrassed. "I kind of blew my load on that first date."

"It was a good first date," I admit, swallowing hard as the back of his hand brushes mine down at our sides. "But this is nice too." I'm not lying for his benefit, either: I've basically grown up on this boardwalk, feeding quarters into the big standing binoculars and eating corn dogs from Skip's on the Beach, but it's different to be here with Clayton—the neon signs glowing just a little bit brighter, the twilight just a little more blue.

"Good." Clayton grins. He's wearing his Tottenham hoodie

again, his skin a full shade tanner than it was the last time I saw him. I tried on basically everything left in my closet before deciding on a low-key sundress and a pair of skinny gold bangles of Nonna's. As outfits go, it's hardly the height of glamour—it's not even a moth-eaten flapper costume—but still it's the fanciest and most grown up I've felt . . . maybe ever. Hanging out with Miles has felt like finding a hidden chapter of a book I've read a million times before, new and exciting. But being with Clayton feels like discovering the lost Library of Alexandria.

We play a few rounds of Skee-Ball in the arcade and poke through a couple of souvenir shops, then pick up dinner at a to-go falafel place that's new this summer and head down to the water to eat. Clayton pulls a blanket out of his backpack—so like, no, it's not a trip to Canada, but clearly the guy planned ahead—and we spread ourselves out on the sand as the sky turns from purple to black.

"I should come down here more," Clayton says, leaning back on his elbows to peer at the moon hanging over the water, his long legs stretched out in front of him. "Do you know I think I've only been on this beach like three times in my entire life?"

"Really?" I ask. "How is that even possible?"

"Just never happened, I guess." He shakes his head. "My parents were more into capital *V* vacations, you know?"

That makes me smile, shaking my head as I unwrap my pita. "Tough life."

Clayton shrugs, though he's mostly lying down so the gesture doesn't totally translate. "I'm not complaining," he says. "I mean, I guess I'm complaining a little bit. It always felt like they probably could have gotten into screaming matches at home just as easily and saved themselves the airfare."

"Yikes." I glance over at him in the darkness, the only light coming from the boardwalk in the distance and the sliver of moon overhead. "They don't get along, I take it?"

"They hate each other's guts."

I blink; I don't know how to answer that, exactly, or how to respond to the cold, factual way he said it. "I'm sure that's not true," I finally say.

Clayton looks at me funny, his whole body getting very still. "How could you possibly be sure about that?"

"I—" That stops me. I think again of that night at the pizza place last year, how I just totally forgot about his family coming in because the way they acted didn't fit in with the picture of them I already had in my head. I think of Bethany sitting across the table the other day: *My life is not perfect, whatever you might think.* "You're right," I tell him truthfully. "I'm sorry. I don't know anything about them."

"They're not monsters," Clayton says—sitting upright now, reaching for his falafel. "They just . . . should probably not be married to each other, that's all." He shrugs. "Anyway, I think that's part of why Bethany felt like she could talk to me about her dad's . . . whatever." He waves his hand vaguely in a way I assume is supposed to communicate *double life and second family.* "She knew I wouldn't judge her."

I nod. "Can I ask what happened with you guys?" I venture. "You and Bethany, I mean?"

Clayton considers that for a moment. "We were on the rocks for a long time," he says finally. "I think, toward the end, we were kind of together because that was what everybody expected, you know? And staying together was easier than rocking the boat." He shrugs again, picking a tomato out of his pita. "But then I started kind of liking someone else, and—"

"Who?" I interrupt, my voice shrill and demanding enough that I wince at the sound of it. Still, the surge of jealousy is instant and uncontrollable. I was prepared for things with Bethany to be complicated, maybe, but not for some mystery third party.

Clayton looks over at me for a moment, the smirk barely perceptible on his face. "Rachel," he says, and his voice is very patient. "Come on."

It takes a moment for the penny to drop, and as soon as it does, I shake my head firmly. "No way," I manage. "Just because we're doing . . . whatever it is we're doing now does not mean you get to rewrite history. You did not break up with Bethany Lewis because you wanted to date me. You never even noticed me until I gave that speech at graduation."

"Never *noticed* you?" Clayton laughs. "Rachel, I hate to tell you this, but like . . . you are very noticeable."

I blink. "I am?"

"I mean, you fully wrote my name on the whiteboard in math class freshman year," Clayton points out gently. "You strolled into

Moxie's and ordered a Scooper Bowl with your skirt stuck up into your underwear. And you almost caused a chemical explosion when you walked in on me and Bethany in the lab last spring." He's smiling at me now, easy and open. "How could I *not* notice you?"

I am . . . vehemently not charmed. "Oh my God," I say, abandoning my falafel and burying my face in my hands. "Oh my *God*. Okay. This has all been great, but if you'll excuse me, I need to go fill my pockets with stones and walk into the lake now."

Clayton reaches out and tries to tug my hands away from my face, but I don't budge. "Why?"

"Are you serious?" I shake my head. "None of those are good things."

"They're charming things," Clayton counters. "They're memorable things." He sighs. "Look, I'd be lying if I said I never realized over the last four years that maybe you had a little crush on me, or whatever."

Holy crap, this is too humiliating. "So what?" I ask, my voice muffled. "You liked that I liked you?"

"Partly," Clayton allows. "But then . . . I don't know. I started watching you back, I guess. And I liked what I saw."

"You did?" I peek out from between my fingers at that, just barely. "Like what?"

Clayton raises his eyebrows knowingly, like *I see you over there fishing for compliments but will allow it this one time.* "How single-minded you were about stuff, first of all," he tells me. "How focused. How you knew exactly what you wanted and weren't afraid to do whatever you needed to do to get it." He shrugs again. "The idea of being the object of all that energy . . . it was kind of sexy."

"In a terrifying way, you mean."

"Don't deflect," he orders quietly. All at once I think of Miles, a little jolt like an electric shock, but then Clayton smiles and I'm not thinking of anything but what's happening right here.

"I'm not," I tell him truthfully. It just takes a minute to get comfortable with the thought of it, that's all: the idea that all the most complicated parts of myself—the same qualities that have been such an asset at school and such a liability in my personal life—might actually be the things Clayton likes most about me. "I'm not."

Clayton nods seriously. "Good," is all he says.

For a moment I think he might be about to kiss me, but instead he just finishes his falafel in what amounts to two giant bites, washing it down with a big swig of pop. "So," he says, sitting back on the blanket and looking at me speculatively, "how's the whole 'summer of yes' thing working out for you?"

I forgot I told him about that; I think about it for a moment. "Well, some jerk convinced me to do a terrifying bungee jump ride," I say finally, eyeing him playfully as I finish my own pita. "But on the whole . . . I'd call the experiment a success."

After dinner we head back to Moxie's for milkshakes, Clayton taking my hand as we cross the boardwalk as naturally as if he's been doing it his entire life. "Look at that," he points out, nodding with his chin across the shop as we glance around for a table. "There's nobody in the phone booth."

"Oh no?" I follow his gaze. He's right: for once it's abandoned, no little kids playing make-believe or couples making it #Moxiesofficial.

"Nope," he says. "Want to check it out?"

I raise my eyebrows, tilting my head and gazing at him. "I'm sorry," I tease, "for what purpose, exactly?"

"One guess," Clayton says, then tugs me inside and shuts the door behind us.

19

The following night I'm ready for Adam's party a full hour before Miles is supposed to pick me up. My whole body feels as tight as the strings inside the piano at Ruoxi's house, like if anyone touched me I might emit an involuntary sound. I have to end things with Miles—being with Clayton again last night made that much abundantly clear—but the thought of actually doing it makes me want to leave for Evanston tonight and beg the dorms to let me in early. I owe him the truth, and I'm going to tell it to him.

I just need to find the right moment.

I'm lurking around the kitchen waiting for my phone to charge when Jackson traipses in. He flops down in a chair at the table and crosses his arms. "You okay?" I ask.

He groans in response.

"So . . . no?" Whoever said girls are more dramatic than boys has never had a twelve-year-old brother. "Jacks, we could play charades or you could just tell me what's up." I glance down as my phone lights up with a text from Carrie confirming Adam's address.

See you soon, I tell her. **I'm bringing Miles along—hope that's cool?**

Three dots trill for a moment, then: **O rly?**

We're just hanging out, I assure her quickly. I don't even know how to begin to explain the situation between me and Clayton and Miles.

Carrie texts the eyebrow raised emoji, the phone buzzing just as Jackson loudly announces, "It's this girl."

I blink. "Okay," I say as calmly as I can manage, not wanting to sound as surprised as I am. "From school?"

Jackson hesitates and then nods.

"And you want *my* advice?" This is a first. Not to mention the fact that I'm probably the very last person who should be giving anyone dating advice. I only just started doing it thirty seconds ago, and I'm already in way over my head.

"Well, I can't ask Mom. Or Nonna . . ." He groans.

"Nonna what?" Nonna says, coming into the kitchen like we've summoned her, needlepoint in hand. I can't help but wonder if she's been waiting in the hallway this whole time like a beloved theater actress waiting for her cue.

Jackson's cheeks redden and he throws his head back against the chair. "Forget it," he says. "It's nothing."

"No no no," I say quickly, eager for the chance to dig into a romantic drama besides my own. "Let us help."

Nonna pours a cup of coffee, glancing back and forth between Jackson and me. "Help with what?" she asks.

"A girl." I wiggle my eyebrows and Nonna gets this huge smile.

"Oh my God," Jackson groans. "Seriously. I never said anything." He gets up and stomps out of the room.

Nonna ignores him, setting up at the table with her needlepoint: a floral pattern this time, I see, plus the words *feminist killjoy.* Have I mentioned today that I love my nonna? "What's with him?" she asks, jerking her head toward the door.

I shrug. "Puberty?"

Nonna laughs. "Fair enough." She peers down through her bifocals at her pattern, then back up at me. "So how about you?" she asks. "You off somewhere exciting tonight?"

"A party, actually," I admit, pleased to be able to tell her. "With Miles."

"Ah, Miles," Nonna echoes, busying herself with her stitching. "You two have been spending a lot of time together lately, it feels like."

"Some," I allow. "We're friends, that's all."

Nonna nods without looking up. "And you're still spending time with that young man from school?" she asks. "The one you went to Canada with, the soccer player?"

"Clayton?" I ask dumbly, like there are just so many gents in my life who fit that particular description that I can't be expected to know which one she means without further clarification. "I saw him last night, yeah."

"Hmm." Nonna keeps her eyes on her embroidery, doesn't miss a stitch, but still there's something in that one simple syllable that says more than Dr. Paula managed to cram into an entire book.

I blow a breath out, already sort of knowing where this is going. "Nonna—"

"I didn't say anything," she cuts me off, holding a hand up. "And I wouldn't say anything. You're young! I'm happy for you. After all this time, you should be getting out and having fun. I just want you to make sure you're being careful, that's all."

I chew on my thumbnail, not liking the trajectory here. "What are you worried about?" I ask, and it comes out a little snottier than I mean for it to. "That I'm going to get some kind of reputation?"

Nonna shoots me a look. "No, Patatina," she says calmly. "I have never in my life worried about a reputation, yours or my own. I'm worried about you getting hurt, that's all. Or, more to the point, you hurting someone else without meaning to."

I frown. There's a part of me that knows she's right—most of me knows she's right, actually; after all, haven't I spent the better part of today tied up in knots over what I'm going to say to Miles? Still, it feels hugely unfair that all of a sudden she's so worried about collateral damage. "You know, you were the one who was always on me about getting out of the house and not being such a loser all the time," I point out. "But now that I'm actually doing it—"

"Who said anything about you being a loser?" Nonna interrupts me. "Sweetheart, that's not what I think at *all*. You're incredible—smart, funny, a world-class Gondola engineer." She shakes her head.

"I wanted you to be open to the world, that's all. Figuring out how to do that and still be true to yourself is just a part of growing up." She pushes her chair out and takes my face in her smooth, papery hands, plants a smacking kiss on my cheek.

"Have a ball tonight," she instructs me. "I can't wait to hear all about it."

20

*A*dam's party is way closer to what I always imagined when I tried to picture how other people were spending their Saturday nights in high school: drunk-sounding laughter and the pulsing bass of a forgettable pop song, the slightly animal smell of too many people in too small a space. Which isn't to say Adam's house is tiny. The opposite, actually: it makes Spencer's look like a summer cottage, with a great room boasting a two-story stone fireplace and what looks like the library from *Beauty and the* freakin' *Beast* visible through a set of wide double doors to one side.

I glance over my shoulder to make sure Miles is following as I weave through the densely packed crowd in search of Carrie, grabbing his wrist a little roughly so he doesn't fall behind. "You okay?" he asks in my ear, and I nod. It's the third time he's asked since he came to pick me up, and I guess I don't blame him: he leaned in to kiss me hello and I feinted, pecking him on the side of the mouth before ducking around him and slipping into the passenger seat of the Civic. Probably I'd be wondering what the heck was up, too, if I were him. Still, the wary way he's watching me, like he's on the lookout for danger, makes me feel trapped and surveilled. I should have just told him the truth up front instead of dragging him to this party he didn't want to go to in the first place, this house full of people neither one of us knows.

I just had no idea what to say.

The kitchen is wall-to-wall bodies, a bunch of liquor bottles on the counter and a cooler full of melting ice on the floor near the wide accordion door. "Keg's on the patio!" announces a guy I don't recognize, offering Miles a drunken high five.

Miles obliges, slapping the guy's palm before trailing me out into the wide, artfully manicured yard. The lawn is crowded with partygoers, the pool so full of people it looks like a human soup. "Where did they all come from?" Miles asks, and I shake my head. "It's like a plague."

Thankfully I spot Carrie a moment later, perched elegantly on the stone ledge at the far end of the patio in shredded jeans and a silky crop top. "Rach!" she squeals, the contents of her red plastic party cup sloshing onto her wrist as she hops down off the wall and hurries over. "You came!"

"Summer of yes," I remind her grimly. "You know Miles, right?" I ask.

"Obviously," she says, drunkenly expansive. She holds her cup up in a toast. "We're old friends."

"The dearest," Miles agrees gamely, though I'm pretty sure the only time they've ever exchanged even the briefest of pleasantries was that day beside the Cream Cart.

"I'm so glad you guys are here. I want you to meet Adam!" Carrie grabs my hand in her free one and hauls me across the patio before I can remind her that we actually already know each other, that even before she reintroduced us at the carnival a couple weeks ago we spent the better part of elementary school in the same class. "Did I already say I'm glad you're here? I'm so glad you're here."

I shoot Miles a look over my shoulder like, *Oh God, please save me.* He makes an exaggerated *I'm sorry, what? I don't understand you* gesture in return that has me laughing in spite of myself. He looks sort of ridiculously cute tonight, if I'm being honest, dressed in jeans a click nicer than the ones he usually wears and a lightweight plaid button-down rolled up to the elbows. His hair, for once, is actually combed. It makes me feel kind of crappy, to think of him getting ready over at his house while I paced mine trying to figure out how best to let him down easy. But that doesn't mean I don't appreciate the effort.

We chat with Adam and his private school buddies for a while—or, more accurately, Carrie chats enough for all of us, her voice loose with that cheerful drunken lilt. Eventually Adam lifts his chin at Miles, nodding in recognition. "Vandenberg," he says. "How you been, dude?"

Miles nods back coolly, an expression on his face I don't entirely recognize and a weird tautness in his shoulders. When I pull him aside a moment later, it's my turn to ask if he's okay.

"Yeah," he says, coming back to himself, "I'm fine. I just didn't realize this was Adam Meyers's house, that's all."

I frown. "Oh." I guess I did actually fail to mention that, now that I think about it, though of course Miles went to school with him when we were kids same as me. "Yeah, why?"

He shrugs. "I mean, that dude beat me up like four times in middle school," he admits. "But other than that, no reason."

My eyes widen. "Seriously?"

"It's fine," Miles assures me with a crooked smile, shaking his head. "I'm over it now. You know, mostly."

"That guy, really?" My mouth drops open at the unfairness of it, outrage on Miles's behalf. "He had a monkey backpack!"

Miles smirks. "Not by eighth grade, he didn't."

"Want me to go beat him up now?" I ask. "As, like, payback?"

He considers that for a moment. "Tempting," he says. "Think you're up for it?"

"I'm very tough." I blow a breath out. "Do you want to leave?" The idea fills me with a weird, perverse hope, actually—we could get out of here; we could have our Talk and get it over with, even if I still don't know exactly what I'm going to say, especially in light of the fact that apparently I've lured him into the lair of his pubescent tormentor—but Miles shakes his head.

"Nah," he says, jamming his hands into his pockets. "You wanted to do this, right? I feel like we're constitutionally obligated to stay here and drink his booze at the very least." He leads me toward the keg, filling a red cup and handing it over. "Bottoms up, princess."

"You're not having one?" I ask, taking a tiny sip and wrinkling my nose at the bitter foam.

"I'm driving," he reminds me, "which means you've got to drink for both of us."

"For your honor," I say solemnly.

"Exactly."

I smile, taking another sip. The thing about Miles is that I actually do have a really good time with him, when I get out of my own way and let myself. There's a part of me that can picture exactly what it would be like for us to be together for real: meeting at home on the weekends this fall and watching movies on the giant projector screen, him joking around with my parents at the restaurant. Fun and familiar and easy and safe.

But also: Clayton.

We do a lap through the crowded house and wind up in the massive basement, which boasts a pool table, a shuffleboard setup, and a Ping-Pong table, which is currently being used for a double-stacked game of beer pong. A crowd of people cheer or clap every few seconds. "You want in?" some dude in a Lions jersey asks Miles, who—to my utter shock—actually seems to consider it.

"I need a base runner," he tells me. "You in?"

"A what?"

"To drain the cups. You up for it?"

I stare at him pointedly. "Are you serious?"

"Don't worry," he says, "you're not going to have to chug a ton of beer or anything." He grins then, suddenly a little wolfish. "I'm really good at this."

"At beer pong?" I make a face but then remember my new mantra. I'm Team Yes, aren't I? I can do this. "Okay," I say. "But you better be as good as you say."

He winks. "I'm better."

To my complete and utter shock, he isn't actually lying; before long, he's attracted a huge crowd. Every time he bounces a ball, it goes in immediately like he's got some kind of preternatural drinking-game ability, the entire basement erupting in cheers. "I'm sorry," I say after a few minutes, nudging him in the shoulder as he accepts a round of fist bumps from Lions Jersey and his buddies. "Are you a secret beer pong savant?"

Miles shrugs in a way that definitely means yes. "Tommy used to always play with our cousins when he was in high school," he explains. "They'd let me play with water cups."

I shake my head. "Speaking of water," I tell him, "I'm going to go grab some." I've probably had less than half a beer, all told, but still my head is the tiniest bit swimmy. "Might check on Carrie too."

Miles nods. "You want me to come with?"

"Nah, you're in your element," I tease, and he rolls his eyes. "You do you."

"I always do," he promises, smiling before turning back to the game. "Hurry back."

✳

It's probably been less than an hour since we got here, but still it seems like the population of the house has more than doubled: I can barely make my way through the kitchen to the patio without being jostled or getting lost. Now that I'm moving around, my head is a little fuzzier than I realized. I scan the yard for Carrie or Adam, but I don't see either one. I've just fired off a **where'd you get to?** text when a hand lands on my lower back.

"Oh hey," Clayton says, his voice in my ear low and deep and private. "I know you."

Oh my God. "Oh my God!" I say, almost dropping my phone on the patio. "Um. Hi!"

"Hi yourself," Clayton says. He looks surprised in a good way— which, I remind myself in a panic, is how I should try to look as well. "What are you doing here?"

"Carrie invited me," I explain. "What are you doing here?"

"Carrie invited Ethan. I'm just crashing."

My phone buzzes inside my hand, a bumblebee sounding an alarm: **In the living room!** Carrie's texted. **Also FYI Clayton is here.**

Yes, thanks, I think wildly, shoving the phone back into my pocket. *I see that.* "Um," I say, trying with little success to come up with some kind of plan that isn't something out of a '90s sitcom, me running back and forth between Clayton and Miles dressed in some kind of corny disguise. "How are you?"

"I'm good," he says with a smile. Then, raising an eyebrow: "You okay?"

"Yup! I'm great." I glance around one more time, making sure Miles hasn't come up here to find me. "Hey, want to go for a walk?" I fan myself with one hand, which isn't actually an affectation, seeing as all of a sudden I can barely breathe. "So many people out here."

Clayton nods. "Sure," he says.

I practically drag him toward the far side of the yard and down the hill, where the property meets the water, the smell of pine trees and water replacing the low-hanging cloud of body spray and beer. There's a long dock there, a speedboat at the end of it. Just for a moment, I imagine taking a running leap and diving behind the wheel, gunning the motor, and speeding off down the creek. Never mind that I have no idea how to drive a boat.

"You sure you're okay?" Clayton asks, nearly tripping over a gnarled tree root before following me out onto the dock.

Oh my God, if one more person asks me that tonight, I'm going to lose it. "I'm good!" I insist, aware that I'm not totally selling it. "Parties just aren't my scene, you know?" None of this is my scene, let's be real; in no universe am I the kind of person to wind up accidentally toggling between two guys in one night like the world's most awkward romantic multitasker.

"I mean, fair enough," Clayton says, sitting down on the dock so his feet dangle a little ways above the water. "Shine starting to wear off the summer of yes?"

I hesitate, glancing back at the house for a moment. I think back to what Nonna said earlier, about making sure nobody gets hurt here. I know I should make an excuse, then dash back into the house, collect Miles the Beer Pong King, and take us both as far away from this place as humanly possible.

Instead, I sit down on the dock beside Clayton. "Kind of," I admit, my hand landing on top of his on the splintery wood.

"That's too bad," Clayton says, pushing his shoulder against mine ever so slightly. When I glance in his direction, he's looking back at me, steady, intent written all over his face.

"Yeah." I can hear the party still raging in the yard—a splash, the sound of someone cackling—but it sounds like it's happening somewhere very far away. "I mean, let's be real, it probably couldn't last forever, right?"

"Probably not," Clayton agrees. "For what it's worth, though? I'm really glad you're here."

That's when he ducks his head and kisses me.

No, no, no, I think, even as I feel myself leaning into him. Holy crap, this is a truly *terrible* idea. I'm supposed to be distracting him, then running away. But it's like all my self-control—and all the uncertainty I've been feeling tonight—has totally dissolved with the hot press of Clayton's mouth.

Yes, I think.

Yes, yes, yes.

I wrap my arms around his neck, twisting to get even closer. Clayton's fingertips ghost along the hem of my tank top, making me gasp. I'm so focused on the feel and smell and taste of him that

I almost don't hear the sound of the dock creaking as somebody else steps onto it: When I open my eyes, there's Miles standing a couple yards away with his hands in his pockets, a look on his face like he's died.

"Yeah," he says, and I will never in my life forget how quiet his voice is. "This seems right."

21

I scramble upright so fast I get dizzy, a splinter from the dock lodging itself in the meat of my palm. "Um," I say, wobbling a little, righting myself again. "Hi."

Miles looks at me, then at Clayton, who's getting belatedly to his feet, then back at me again. "What the hell do you think you're doing?" he asks.

"Whoa." Clayton's eyes narrow, protective. "Take it easy, bro."

"I'm not your bro," Miles says, dark eyes still locked on mine. "Are you *kidding* me?" His voice cracks a little here, rough and ragged. "Like, in all honesty—what the hell, Rachel?"

"I—" I break off, utterly useless. After all, I have no excuse. I was kissing Clayton. I wanted to be kissing Clayton. If Miles hadn't interrupted us, I would probably still be kissing Clayton.

"What the hell did you bring me here for?" Miles continues.

"What the hell was the point of any of this, if you just wanted to . . . I mean, if you were also—"

"I'm sorry," I say, and it comes out like begging. "I'm so sorry. I was going to talk to you tonight. I just—"

"Wait," Clayton says. I watch his face change as it registers, the pieces finally clicking into place. "You guys came here together?"

"Among other things," Miles says, his voice cold. "Bro."

"Like, *together*-together?"

"Is that so difficult to believe?" Miles snaps.

"No, dude, I just—" Clayton shakes his head, looking at me. "Really?"

Both of them are looking at me now, waiting for an explanation. There's no getting out of this. I take a deep breath. "Yes."

Miles just shakes his head, but Clayton turns on me. "What the hell, Rachel? You're on a *date* right now?"

"I—" I scramble for a way to defend myself. "Look," I manage, holding my hands up like I'm some kind of calm, reasonable third party here, "it's not like either one of you is— I mean, guys do this all the time, right? Play the field or whatever?"

"Oh, no fucking way," Miles says immediately. "This is not, like, an issue of feminism."

Clayton shakes his head. "What was all that shit about me and Bethany?" he demands. "That whole time you were doing the *exact* same thing you got so mad at me for, except I wasn't even actually doing it!"

"I—" I break off one more time. They're right; I know they're right. I didn't mean for any of this to happen. I never wanted anyone to get hurt. But I spent so long saying no to everything that when I started hanging out with both of them—when I *liked* both of them, and they both liked me back—I couldn't bring myself to make a choice.

It just all spiraled out of control.

"I'm so sorry," I tell them truthfully, swallowing down the threat of tears at the back of my throat. "If you can let me try to explain—"

"Don't bother," Miles says flatly. Clayton just shakes his head.

I feel all the air whoosh out of me then, a parachute collapsing. I know there's no excuse for what I pulled here, and from looking at their faces, I know it's all over. Miles gazes at me for another moment, then turns and heads back toward the party. Clayton hesitates half a beat longer. I reach for his arm to stop him but he shrugs my hand away and just like that he's gone too, leaving me more alone than I've felt all summer.

More alone than I've felt in my life.

I plunk back down on the dock, digging at the splinter wedged deep in my palm and letting the tears come quick and overwhelming. I can't believe this happened. I can't believe I made such a freaking mess. It feels like I'm under an interrogation light, with everything I've been trying to keep hidden finally exposed for the entire world to see.

No. Wait.

I don't just feel like it.

I actually *am* caught in the beam of a spotlight.

I blink, wiping my swollen eyes as the brightness washes over me, then the rest of the dock and up over the party, cutting through the darkness like a knife. A voice booms over a loudspeaker: "This is the police," it announces officiously, echoing out over the water. "Everyone stay where you are." Both the voice and the spotlight are coming from a boat on the lake.

Suddenly, there are also a bunch of blue and red flashing lights coming from every direction—all across the water and up the single drive to the house. The police. Chaos erupts all around me as the people on the lawn, in the gazebo, and on the porch begin to scramble in every direction. "Run!" someone shouts.

Run where? We're basically on an island—surrounded now by police boats, plus three cars pulling into the driveway. There's nowhere to go, unless I want to make a swim for it—which a few people actually do, careening past me and diving off the end of the dock, but they get caught in the spotlight of the boat cops pretty much immediately.

"Get out of the water," the voice booms.

In the confusion, all around me people take off toward the house, but I can only stand there, dumbstruck. If we try to run, won't we just get into more trouble? I look around everywhere for Carrie. Or Clayton. Or Miles. But I don't see any of them. Instead, I see a bunch of really drunk and dazed-looking people all being herded to an area near the front drive, by the garage doors. Several are sopping wet and a few more are still scrambling from the various officers, trying to hide or get away however they can without much success.

Suddenly a heavy hand comes down on my shoulder. I look up at the police officer it belongs to. "Come with me," he says.

Just when I thought this night couldn't get any worse.

22

*O*f all the ways I thought this night might end, getting arrested by boat cops was not even remotely on the list of possibilities.

I lean my head against the backseat of my parents' staid sedan, the silence thick as fog as I stare at nothing out the window. The police made every minor who wanted to leave Adam's property either take a Breathalyzer test and blow a perfect 0.0, or come with them back to the station to be collected by their parents. Since both Miles and Clayton could blow 0, they were allowed to leave—which both of them did without even the slightest glance in my direction—but because I'd been the beer pong base runner, I knew I couldn't pass the test.

So here I am.

Neither Mom nor Dad says anything the whole ride home, which is actually worse than if one or both of them had ripped me a new one. They're so angry they can't even speak. It feels like waiting for a storm cloud to break, knowing you're about to be deluged. Realizing too late you left your umbrella at home.

Once we get into the house, they steer me directly into the kitchen, parking me at the table before sitting down across from me. Neither of them has said a single word.

My mom rakes her hands through her hair, looks at me for a moment. "What were you *thinking*?" she asks.

And oh, here comes the rain.

She goes on for a solid ten minutes about her disappointment and the poor example I'm setting for Jackson. About how she doesn't recognize me anymore. About how she's worried that I'm going to go completely off the rails when I go away next month and throw away everything I've worked so hard for: "Am I going to get a call from the coroner in Evanston?" she finishes, her voice breaking. "To come identify your *body*?"

My *body*? Even through my haze of guilt and shame and regret, that seems a little bit ridiculous and needlessly dramatic, though obviously I know better than to point that out. But it must be visible on my face, because Mom shakes her head. "One stupid move is all it takes, you know? You get drunk and fall into a pool and drown. The end."

"Mom," I try, "I didn't actually get drunk—"

"I. Am. Not. Finished," she says. It's clipped and aggressive. Anger in staccato.

I glance at my dad, who keeps his eyes trained on my mom. If I were expecting a sympathetic look, I won't find it there. Not from him. And definitely not tonight.

"I just don't know what's gotten into you." She throws up her hands. "You can't leave the house. Ever."

I bark an incredulous laugh; I can't help it. Mom whirls on me like a lioness, but Dad lays a hand on her arm. "Let's all just take a breath," he begins.

"I don't want to take a breath!" my mom fires back, surprising me. "I don't feel like being reasonable. I feel like keeping her safe. Protected."

I bite my lip and glance between Mom and Dad. It's as if they've forgotten I'm here, witness to this conversation. All of a sudden, it feels like maybe this is about way more than me and tonight's disaster; all at once it occurs to me that my mom and I have more in common than I ever thought. My fear was of rejection, of emotional pain, I think, not the fear of drowning or God only knows what dark thoughts Mom's batting around in her head. But the point remains: We've both spent way too much time allowing ourselves to be directed by fear. "Mom—" I try again, but she cuts me off.

"Don't." She shakes her head. "I mean it, Rachel."

"Don't *what?*" I counter, anger flaring. "You're just not going to let me talk at all ever again? That's your new parenting strategy?"

"Okay!" Dad holds up both hands like a referee. "Clearly we're all feeling a little bit fraught here," he says gently.

"Do not patronize me," Mom snaps, and I realize with a start that she's on the verge of tears. "I don't understand why I'm the only one who sees where this is headed. I *lived* through this already; don't you two get that? My *mother* lived through this. And I will do whatever it takes to keep Rachel from . . . from . . ."

"From *what*, exactly?" I ask, though of course I already know the answer. Of course I know the answer. She wants to keep me from making the same mistake she made.

"From making a mistake like having me."

It never mattered how well I did in school, I realize suddenly. It never mattered how many rules I followed, how much I achieved. My mom was always going to be afraid I would end up just like her: a victim of the kind of dumb, impetuous choices that derailed her entire life.

Already Mom is shaking her head, reaching her hand across the table: "That's *not* what I meant," she starts, but I can barely hear her over the roaring in my ears.

"I'm not you," I tell her, setting my jaw even as my eyes blur. Then I shake my head and rush out of the room.

My mom makes a sound then, almost a whimper: *"Rachel,"* she starts, shoving her chair back and calling after me.

But I'm already gone.

23

I spend all night and most of the following day in the kind of miserable, restless not-sleep I associate with having a fever: all pounding head and muscle aches, the blankets tangled around my feet. I just keep replaying the events of last night over and over like some horrifying boomerang.

Clayton hates me. Miles hates me. My mom probably hates me. And I don't think I can fix it.

Around two in the afternoon, there's a knock on my bedroom door, and Nonna pokes her head in. "Can I come in?" she asks.

I nod into my pillow.

She walks in and sets a plate with a sandwich on my bedside table. I haven't eaten all day, but I'm not hungry. Then she slides up next to me on the bed, the big spoon to my little, and I completely break down.

"Patatina." Nonna runs her fingers through my hair and gathers it off the nape of my neck like she used to when I was little, the citrus and juniper smell of her enough to have me crying even harder. "You know, I've been watching you this summer. You've been very unlike yourself lately."

"That was the point," I tell her, my voice muffled into the pillows. "I wanted to be someone new."

"But why, sweetheart?" she asks. "Why do you think you need to change anything about yourself?"

"Because I am a boring, friendless loser," I manage to spit out between heaves.

"*Cazzate,*" she says. *Bullshit.* I snort, and because of the tears it comes out much moister than I intend. I sound like an actual hog spluttering in its trough.

"I mean it, my girl. Enough with the loser talk. I don't care for it. You are a beautiful person, inside and out. Your heart is your best attribute, your brain a very close second."

I roll my eyes. "You're my grandma. You have to say that."

I can feel her shake her head against my neck. "Nope. I don't *have* to say anything. I'm old. I do what I want."

"You aren't old."

"Well, I've never been one to hold my tongue, either." She tightens her embrace around me. "So, do you want to tell me what exactly happened? The real story, not your parents' version."

"You heard that one already, huh?"

She laughs. "I'm pretty sure the entire neighborhood heard it." Then she sighs. "Come on, my love. Out with it."

So I take a deep breath and tell her everything: about Miles and Clayton at the party, the look in their eyes when they figured it all out. About Spencer's party and Dine Around and the wind in my hair on the drive up to Canada; about clearing the air with Carrie and listening to Bethany talk about her dad.

About how scared I was of rejection, and what it felt like to realize that so is everyone else.

"I felt like I spent all of high school saying no to stuff because I thought I already knew it would be terrible," I explain, finally rolling over to face her. "So when I found your book, it seemed like a sign."

Nonna frowns. "What book?"

I gesture to it on the nightstand. "That one. *A Season of Yes!*"

"Huh." She grabs the book, then sits up, turning Dr. Paula's magnum opus over in her hands to examine it.

I push myself up onto my elbows. She doesn't remember the book? How could she not? She's got notes scribbled in the margins; the pages are dog-eared. It looks like the sort of well-worn tome that must've meant something to her, that must have served as a guidebook that got her where she is today. Nonna flips through a few pages and then groans when the recognition finally hits. *"Marone,"* she says, *"this* book?"

"Yes, this book. I've been applying Dr. Paula's process to my life this summer."

"Saying yes to *every* opportunity?" she asks.

I nod. "Pretty much."

222 LINDSEY ROTH CULLI

"Oh, Patatina. Not this book." She buries her face in her hands.

What? What is she talking about? "But all of your notes? In the margins? You underlined so much!"

"This book is how I lost my second husband, gained forty pounds, and almost lost my house."

What? My eyes widen and my heart races. "What do you mean? Why did you keep it, then?"

"I don't know, honestly. I like surrounding myself with books, I guess. I keep them all." Nonna points to the picture of Dr. Paula. "She should have said no to those glasses, I can tell you that much." She laughs and tosses the book off the bed. "Listen to me, my love. Despite your protests, I am actually old. It's not a dirty word! I embrace it, wrinkles and all, because it represents the life I've lived, the life I've *loved*. But, when I was young, I made mistakes and learned from them. Sometimes those mistakes were because of some idea I got in my head, some self-help book's suggestion, or sometimes because I just plain goofed up."

She pulls me into her side and presses my head against her shoulder. "Oh, my girl, I want you to make mistakes, make a whole mess of them. Because getting yourself out of a pickle is how you will learn and grow. If everything always works out perfectly according to your plan every time, you'll miss so many chances for surprise and adventure." She gestures toward the book. "But clearly Dr. Paula Prescott has never heard of opportunity costs."

"Opportunity costs?"

"In economics." She pats my hand. "When you say yes to

something, you are inherently saying no to almost everything else. Unless this Dr. Paula has also figured out how to be in two places at once and also taught you that skill?" I smile weakly and shake my head.

"Every choice has embedded within it an opportunity cost. Saying yes isn't free. When you said no to parties and to boys, you were saying yes to your family, and to your friends, and to your responsibilities. And sometimes that—learning when to say no and especially what to say no to—is just as important."

"Like to two boys?" I joke.

Nonna nods. "Like I said, you're allowed to be interested in more than one thing, in more than one person, but once the line blurs between casual and committed, especially if you know it's blurred for someone else, you've got to be honest and up front. I mean, you can't literally say yes to two spouses, right?"

"God, Nonna! No one is talking about marriage."

"No, I know that. You're not getting married for a decade. At least." She narrows her eyes at me. "But eventually you have to say no to someone, right? Saying no to one person enables you to say yes to someone else. Eventually. Many, many, many years from now." She shrugs. "I think balance is the key to finding out what you really, actually want. Not just what you're forcing yourself to say yes to."

Maybe she's right.

"It's not all bad, this book. These past several weeks you've been carefree in a way you haven't since you were small." Nonna runs her fingers through my hair, starting a braid crown. "You think I don't notice, that I don't see, but I do. And I know that for such a long time you've been holding yourself together so that even if everything else in the world went wrong, at least your mom wouldn't have to worry about you."

Nonna pulls the strands tight as she loops them into a braid around my head. She tugs me back with her as she leans toward my dresser so she can grab a band and a bobby pin without letting go. "My hope for you is that when you're out on your own, you'll finally feel freed from that burden. It was never yours to carry. And besides, your mom is in a good place now. We are all of us in a good place."

Great. I am full on crying again, trying not to move my head so that Nonna doesn't have to start over. "You're right," I say between sniffles. Of course she's right. I think part of the reason I worked so hard, stayed on the course, and said no to things was because I didn't want to upset my mom or worry her. I couldn't change what my father did, but at the very least, I could make sure I didn't fail her. "I know we are."

That's when someone clears their throat in the doorway: "There room for one more on that bed?" my mom asks, wiping her own damp face with the back of one hand.

"Always," Nonna says, letting out a quiet *oof* as she shifts on the mattress. "See?" she tells me, gesturing down at herself. "Old."

I ignore her. "How long have you been standing there?" I ask my mom.

"Long enough." She crosses the carpet and squishes in between Nonna and me, her corona of dark hair brushing my cheek. "I wasn't trying to eavesdrop, but I need you to understand that you were never, ever a burden. And you were not a mistake." She grabs my cheeks in her hands. "You are one of the greatest joys of my life. I wouldn't change my past, because as hard as that all was, it brought me you."

I swallow what feels like a balled-up pair of socks wedged at the back of my throat. "Really?"

She smiles through her own tears. "Absolutely. And I'm sorry if you ever, *ever* felt like you had to protect me. I was the one trying to protect you."

And now we're crying and hugging and Nonna wraps her arms around both of us, holding us all together in that way she always does. "I'm sorry about last night too. I hate that I made you and Dad worry," I say between sniffs. "I promise that it won't happen again."

Mom hugs me tighter to her chest. "I don't know that you can promise that. But you can promise to try to make better choices, okay?"

"And when you make mistakes, to learn from them," Nonna adds.

"Deal."

"So what's this about a self-help book?" Mom asks, releasing me from the embrace. Nonna and I exchange glances and laugh, and I fill Mom in on everything that went down the last few weeks. To her credit, Mom doesn't even wince when I tiptoe over some of the more embarrassing parts.

"Wow. Well, I'm glad you learned these important life lessons before you were no longer under my roof." She shakes her head. "But if you want to go back to saying no more often, I'd be okay with that."

Nonna clicks her teeth and nudges her shoulder into Mom's. "Apple doesn't fall far from the tree."

"Nut doesn't fall far from the bush," Mom counters immediately, nudging Nonna back. "So what happened with the boys, though?"

Ugh. "Miles and Clayton?"

Mom's eyebrows shoot up. "Miles. As in Vandenberg?"

"That's the one." I nod and throw myself back against the pillows. "I don't think I'll have to say no to either of them anymore."

Nonna shrugs. "Maybe. Maybe not." There's a suggestion in her tone, one that most anyone else wouldn't pick up on but I know Nonna. And I know when I'm being chastened.

"But I do need to apologize," I say, answering the question Nonna hasn't asked.

Mom and Nonna nod together. "Oh, definitely. And no matter what you decide or how you proceed, be kind to both of them," Nonna says.

I sigh. "I know." The trouble is, it doesn't much matter which of them I want to be with. At this point, I'm pretty sure neither of them want anything to do with me.

And I can't say I blame either one.

24

I'm pretty sure that when Dr. Paula was encouraging her readers to open themselves up to new experiences, she didn't mean filling out gym membership forms with fake information as part of a top-secret recon mission. Still, I like to think she'd be proud if she wandered out of the locker room at Club Fit dressed in full '80s Jazzercise regalia and saw me today.

Let's be clear, I have zero intention of joining this torture cult—physical fitness is a bridge too far, even for my summer of yes—but with only a few days before I'm due to pack up and leave for Northwestern, I am running out of options, and quick. Clayton hasn't answered any of my phone calls. He won't return any of my texts. I went to his house, but the driveway was empty, and while some—okay, most—people might argue that his silence is an answer in itself, I can't face the idea of heading off to college without doing absolutely everything I can to try and repair things. Or at least explain myself.

Which is how I wound up here—dutifully pretending to be even remotely interested in toning my biceps, dropping Clayton's name as the person who referred me. "Do you happen to know if he already came by today?" I ask as nonchalantly as I can manage.

A few keystrokes later and the front desk attendant—Jennifer, according to her name badge—looks back up. "He's here right now, actually." She glances around the front area, which is all cardio equipment. "If you don't see him out here, he's probably in the weight room."

Jackpot.

She offers me a tour, but I shake my head. "You know, on second thought, I'm going to pass on the membership. Thanks, though!" I offer her my brightest, sanest smile before darting out of the gym before she can process what's just happened. It's the most running I've done all summer, and by the time I flop down on a nearby bench to wait I'm breathing hard.

I brought a book—fiction this time, thank you (I'm done with self-improvement for a while)—but I keep having to read the same line over and over again, glancing up every thirty seconds to see if he's coming. I scratch at a mosquito bite on my ankle. I think for the hundredth time about giving up and going home.

I've been lurking on my bench for the better part of an hour when finally the sliding doors of the gym whoosh open and Clayton and Ethan stroll out, both of them dressed in mesh shorts and

T-shirts with their backpacks slung over one shoulder. They look like an American Eagle ad, poster boys for the fresh air of Western Michigan and genetically modified corn.

God, what do I think I'm *doing*?

Ethan sees me first, a knowing smirk spreading across his face as he nudges Clayton with one elbow. "Gotta go," he says cheerfully, offering an exaggerated salute before peeling off in the direction of the parking lot. Then, more loudly: "'Sup, Walls?"

Clayton looks in my direction at the sound of my name, his face going on a real emotional journey at the sight of me: surprise, annoyance, trepidation. Back around to annoyance again. He glances at Ethan's retreating back, like he's hoping for reinforcement. Then he scrubs a hand through his hair and sighs. "What do you want, Rach?"

It's a simple question with a complicated answer. I could just let Clayton go off to Milwaukee hating my guts. He doesn't owe me absolution. But I owe him. Even if he won't hear me out. "You're ignoring my texts," I tell him, springing up off the bench and crossing the distance between us, choosing for the moment to focus on the nickname and not the tone behind it.

"I wish you'd just leave me alone."

"I'm going to, I promise. I just needed to talk to you first, and I couldn't get a hold of you any other way."

"Yeah, well." Clayton starts walking again, crossing the patch of grass that leads toward the sidewalk and heading down Main Street in the opposite direction of DiPasquale's. Oh my God, did he walk all the way here from his house? Is he one of those people who runs *to* the gym? "Most people would take the hint."

"That . . . is true," I agree, jogging a little to keep up with him. "But I'm not most people."

Clayton snorts a little. "That's a fact." He's quiet for a moment, just the sound of cars on the road and a baby crying on the Ground Up patio. Then he glances at me out of the corner of his eye. "So," he says without breaking his stride, "talk."

"Oh!" Holy crap, this guy is a fast walker. Already I'm a little out of breath. "Okay. Um. Well, first of all, I wanted to apologize," I tell him, trying not to sound like a fish gasping for water. "For lots of things, but especially for being a hypocrite and for not being honest about, well, a lot."

Clayton nods, just barely. "Okay," he says, still not slowing.

"I've liked you for forever, Clayton," I say, keeping my brisk pace. "I mean, you have to know that. You basically *told* me you knew that. I liked you so much that when it seemed like maybe you actually liked me back, my brain just shorted out with all the reasons why that probably couldn't be a real thing that was happening. I acted like a maniac, just to try and keep myself from getting hurt. And at the same time I was reading this demented book and trying to say yes to everything, even when it started to feel like maybe all the yes-saying was making me do things I didn't want to do and forget who I actually was, but the truth is I'm the same person I've always been."

Clayton glances in my direction, raising an eyebrow. "And who's that, exactly?"

"Kind of a no person," I admit, fully wheezing now. Ugh, I should have joined the gym after all. "Kind of awkward. Kind of a mess."

In the back of my head, it occurs to me that I'm feeling a little bit light-headed; dark spots dance in front of my eyes. Still, I'm determined to get this all out. "For the longest time, I had this idea of you in my head, and I thought there was no way you'd live up to it. But then the real person turned out to be even better than I'd imagined. And he—you—didn't deserve to be treated the way I treated you."

Clayton slows and finally stops where he's standing; he looks at me for a long moment. "Rachel," he says, just the two quiet syllables.

That's when I keel over in the grass in front of the village hall.

※

When I open my eyes, Clayton's kneeling beside me on the grass, a bottle of water in one hand and a granola bar in the other. "Drink this," he instructs, holding the water up to my lips.

I take a messy gulp and wipe my mouth with the back of my hand, still dizzy. "I think my heart exploded," I announce.

Clayton looks at me. "I . . . don't think that's what happened."

"It might be," I argue.

"I doubt it," he says.

"You're a fast walker."

"I'm impressed you kept up."

"Yeah, well." I take a deep breath, another sip of the water. "It was important. Because I really am sorry. And I couldn't stand the idea of you leaving without knowing that."

Clayton stands and reaches out his hand to help me to my feet. I know I must look like a horror show, red-faced and sweaty. Still, I can't help but notice that he doesn't seem to mind. "So when do you take off for Evanston?"

"Soon." But not soon enough, honestly. "You still leaving next week?"

Clayton nods. "Going to be weird, you know? Not being here." He glances around the lawn of the village hall, the place where he, like me, has spent every childhood Fourth of July stretched out on a picnic blanket eating bomb pops and watching the annual parade.

"Will you miss it?" I ask.

"Some things, yeah." He takes a deep breath and lets it out slowly. "But also, I think I'm ready to move on."

I nod, thinking how this could be the last time we're ever together like this. "Well, I'm glad I finally got to know you, Clayton Carville."

Clayton looks at me for a moment. "Me too," he says softly. His face breaks into a grin. "See you around, Rachel Walls."

25

*M*iles calls in sick to work the following day. "Stomach flu," my dad reports, keying an order into the register before calling over his shoulder: "Two boats! Italian combo with hots, plus a pig and Swiss." He turns back to me. "Can you handle the Cream Cart on your own?"

"Sure thing," I promise, though it turns out the shift feels endless without Miles there to crack jokes and benignly annoy me the whole time. I think about texting him—*having a shitty time, wish you were here*—but something tells me he probably wouldn't answer.

Once I'm finally done, I walk home to shower off the gelato, taking my time as I pass by the shops along the strip near DiPasquale's: Mr. Thompson's antique store, Ground Up, that dicey bar on the corner of Main that's always open when it seems like it should be closed and closed when you'd think it would be open. It's weird to think that these are all places I've known forever, places I've seen every day for basically my entire life, and in a few short weeks, I won't see them anymore. For years I've been counting down the days until I could leave, and now that it's actually almost here, I realize how badly I'm going to miss all of it.

Once I'm showered and dressed, I fuss with my hair for a while in front of the bathroom mirror, pick at the beginning of a zit on my chin. It's only when I'm wondering idly if I should get highlights that I realize I'm fully stalling. I take a deep breath, then head downstairs and out the front door toward Miles's.

It takes less time than I expect to get over there, and I stop short a few houses down—stretching my arms and legs like a runner about to start a marathon, trying to psych myself up a little. This is a new experience for me. One by-product of never really doing much of anything is that you never really do that much *wrong*, either. When it comes to apologizing—just like basically everything else in life—I don't have a ton of experience. There's never been that much of a need.

Until now.

Now I'm doing it for the second time in as many days. Finally I tell myself to stop being such a weenie—after all, no matter what else has happened between us or what will happen, it's still *Miles*—and knock on the Vandenbergs' front door. It feels like ages before I hear Miles's footsteps on the other side, cautious; he's obviously hesitating, so I knock again. "I know you're in there," I say.

Finally he opens the door halfway, staring at me from the threshold. "We don't want any," he says flatly.

"Very funny." I shrug then, a little bit helpless. "I messed up."

Miles tilts his dark head to the side, considering that for a moment. "I mean, yeah," he says, not quite looking at me. "Pretty much."

"I didn't respect you. I didn't think about your feelings. I wanted so badly to say yes to everything this summer that I, like, turned into this experience-gobbling monster, and you were just, like . . . one of the things that got gobbled up."

"Seriously?" Miles looks almost amused by how bad I am at this. "'Sorry I gobbled you up like a giant monster'?"

"I'm trying, okay? I'm not good at this!" I protest, laughing a little, but then the laugh turns into something else halfway out and suddenly it feels like I might burst into tears right here on Miles's front porch, site of any number of lemonade stands and snowsuit adjustments and homemade ice pops consumed side by side.

"Look," I tell him, "I made so many stupid mistakes this summer. Honestly, I was trying to figure out a lot of things. Things about myself. Things about life in general. But none of that is an excuse, because the biggest mistake I made was hurting you. I *hate* that I hurt you. And I am so, so sorry."

Miles crosses his arms over his chest, his attention wandering across the street. I turn around and follow his gaze. A car is pulling into Bethany's driveway. We watch as Mrs. Lewis—at least, a woman about Julie's age who I assume is Mrs. Lewis—pulls a couple of grocery bags out of the trunk, running her fingers through her ashy blond hair before straightening her shoulders and heading inside. Even from all the way across the street, she looks gaunt and exhausted.

"Okay." Miles blows a breath out, his shoulders slumping. "As long as we're being honest about our monstrous tendencies here, I guess I should probably tell you something too."

I raise an eyebrow, tuck my hands into the back pockets of my shorts. "Okay?"

He pauses a minute and sits down on the stoop. "The truth is . . . it's possible I knew more about what was going on—or, like, what wasn't going on—between Bethany and Clayton than I necessarily told you."

I blink. "Meaning what, exactly?" I sit down next to him.

He nods toward Bethany's house. "I mean, I don't know *everything*, but obviously there's some kind of giant domestic implosion happening over there. That night Clayton came over, there had been all kinds of theatrics—like her dad's clothes getting thrown out on the lawn, my mom all worked up about whether she should call the cops, that kind of thing. And then later on I saw Bethany and Clayton hanging out on the porch, and . . . I don't know. It didn't seem particularly romantic. They weren't, like, canoodling or anything. They basically just sat out there eating chips."

I tilt my head, wanting to make sure I'm absolutely clear about this. "So you knew there wasn't anything going on between Bethany and Clayton—"

"I mean, I didn't *know*, exactly," Miles says testily. "But yeah. I was pretty sure."

"And you purposely told me that story in a way that made it sound like the other thing?" The anger blooms inside me like some kind of grotesque late-summer flower, huge and red. *"Why?"*

"Why do you *think*, Rachel?" Miles looks at me like I'm completely dense.

I cross my arms and shake my head, not because I don't know the answer but because of course I do: He did it because he liked me enough that he told himself it justified doing something shady. Same as I did what I did because I liked him. "Still, though." I stamp my foot a little, thinking of everything that lie set into motion. "Still."

"Yeah, well, like I said." Miles rolls his eyes, though he doesn't look nearly as disaffected as I think he's probably intending. "Turns out I'm kind of a monster too."

I sigh, knowing we're not actually that different, me and Miles: Both of us are instinctively, reflexively *no* people. Both of us have our reasons. And it's probably past time for both of us to grow up. "You're not a monster," I tell him, raking my hands through my hair. "I mean, don't get me wrong, this totally sucks to hear and I'm super pissed you did it, but it's not any worse than what I did." I shrug. "And maybe I'm not a monster either. I don't know."

"Nah," Miles says immediately, but he's smiling now, just a little. "You're definitely a monster."

"Funny guy." I shake my head. It occurs to me that other than Ruoxi, Miles is probably the best friend I've got. I could just leave it at that, right? Just be the good friends we've always been and go our separate ways. Especially because if I take this step and tell him how I felt—how I still feel—it could implode spectacularly and I could lose him. For keeps this time. The idea of losing Clayton was painful . . . but losing Miles? That would be devastating. But if Dr. Paula's book has taught me anything, it's that sometimes you have to take risks to reap rewards. Or something like that.

"So, are we cool?" Miles asks.

I bite my lip and nod. "We are. But I was actually hoping we could be . . . more than cool." I steal a glance at him.

Miles snorts. "So ice cold, then?"

I reach out with one toe and kick him gently in the ankle. "Don't deflect," I tell him softly, shifting a little so I'm closer to him. "You know what I mean." And I know this is it. Does he want to take this leap with me? Or just leave things as they are?

Miles studies me for another moment. "Yeah," he says, scooting to close the gap between us further. He reaches for my hand then, his thumb skating over the sensitive skin on the inside of my wrist, tracing the veins there. A slow, easy grin spreads across his face. "I think I do."

26

"*I* cannot believe I leave for one summer and you hook up with Clayton freaking *Carville*," Ruoxi says, throwing herself backward into the pillows.

"And Miles Vandenberg," Carrie adds. She and Carrie are sprawled out on the bed watching me pack the last few things I'll need for this year: hair ties and paper clips, all the tiny detritus of my life at home. "We mustn't forget Miles Vandenberg."

"I would never forget Miles Vandenberg," Ruoxi says solemnly. That's when the two of them both crack up.

I smile. I had to say goodbye to Miles yesterday. He got an internship at a small game developer and is going to work there during this semester while he takes a couple classes. "It's not the white hats, but it's pretty cool," he said. I'm actually super-proud of him, but I wish he were still here to see me off.

"Go ahead, have a giggle," I tell them, tossing a turban towel in their general direction, but I'm delighted to have them both here. The two of them seem to have fallen back in step as easily as Carrie and I did. As if both nothing and everything changed.

Carrie twists the wrap around her head while Ruoxi paws through a stack of books that didn't make the cut to bring with me. "What's this?" she asks, holding up *A Season of Yes!,* which has apparently been hiding under the bed for a few weeks now.

I groan even as she starts flipping through it. "A terrible book."

"Oh my God, Rachel." Recognition flashes across Carrie's face as she peers over Ruoxi's shoulder. "This was you. This summer. Wasn't it?"

"No," I say sheepishly. The flush in my cheeks betrays me. "Okay, yes. I tried it."

"And?" Ruoxi raises her dark eyebrows.

"And . . ." I think about it for a moment: Clayton and Carrie and jumping into the pool with my clothes on, dressing up in flapper costumes and getting picked up by the cops. Speeding down highways and crossing over borders. Coming back home again. Miles.

"I'm glad I did it," I say.

Carrie reads out loud: " 'Your present self is built upon what you said yes to yesterday, your future self upon what you choose to say yes to *now.* At your core, you are a product of your past decisions.' Um, that actually sounds super interesting." Carrie tucks the book into her bag. "Mind if I borrow it?"

I smile and shrug. "I mean, sure. But use at your own risk, et cetera."

Carrie grins. "I always do."

It's true that Dr. Paula didn't always know exactly what she was talking about. But as I watch my two friends with their heads ducked close, I'm thankful for the yesses that got me here. That they got us here. Together.

27

*T*wo nights before I'm due to leave for Northwestern, Nonna slides a long, small box across the kitchen table in my direction. "Your graduation present," she explains.

I frown, then look up at her and over at Mom and Dad. "I graduated months ago."

"Okay," she says, "so it's also your birthday present. And your Christmas present. And Rosh Hashanah."

"We're not Jewish," I remind her. "Also, people don't exchange gifts for High Holy Days."

Nonna ignores me. "Chinese New Year," she continues, obviously enjoying herself now. "Arbor Day. Basically this is your present for every holiday for, oh, about the next millennia."

What on earth? The only thing I can think is jewelry—a pearl necklace?—and as Nonna knows, I am not exactly an "adorn your neck with the excrement of oysters" kind of girl. "Nonna, you've already done so much for me."

She waves her hand. "Spend it now or spend it after I'm dead. I choose now, if it's all the same to you. That way I can witness the joy that comes from it."

I ignore the meaning of her words since she's obviously going to live forever and take care to open the package, worried that something very delicate and obviously expensive will come spilling out. But inside the box is only a random key. I narrow my eyes, trying to figure out what it's a key for. And then I see the Toyota emblem.

"No." This is some kind of joke. "A *car*?" I can't even form a full sentence right now, much less verbalize a coherent thought. "You got one? For me?"

"Yes." Nonna clasps her hands. "Don't get too excited—it's definitely nothing fancy, but it will get you from point A to point B. And maybe from point B to point C on occasion too." She winks exaggeratedly in case I'm not catching her meaning that point C equals Detroit. And Miles.

Nonna smiles, and Mom and Dad smile too. "Patatina, you work so hard and I know you were saving up. I thought maybe this way we'd get to see you more."

"And save ourselves six hours of driving every time," Jackson pipes in. Normally I'd glare at him, but instead I just beam.

Nonna grabs my hand and leads me out the back door toward

the garage. There, inside waiting, is a tidy white Corolla. My car. "I'll admit, she's not much, but she's all yours."

"Four doors and a running motor," Dad says. "New brakes, new battery, new tires. The rest of her is ancient, though."

I open the door with the key fob—they keep insisting it's not a very nice car, but it's nice enough to have one of those, plus power locks and windows—and climb into the driver's seat. Despite the small tears in the upholstery and the well-worn steering wheel, there's a sunroof and a decent-looking stereo.

And—oh yeah—it's *mine.*

"We're still driving with you to school, obviously," Mom tells me, "but this way you'll have more opportunities to come back. To us. Home." She looks up and blots the corner of her eyes with her thumb. Dad laughs at her, but when I catch his eye, I find he's choking back tears too.

"Here come the waterworks," Nonna says, nudging my shoulder with a smile.

I beat my family to Evanston by a solid twenty minutes because Jackson has a bladder the size of a walnut and they had to stop. Twice. When I pull into the parking lot, I spot a familiar face in the crowd of dazed-looking freshmen. Miles. He's nonchalantly waiting outside my new residence hall, familiar as home in his black T-shirt and jeans.

His eyes widen when he recognizes me behind the wheel of the

Corolla: "You . . . got a car?" he calls, his voice deep and surprised through the open window.

I jump out and practically tackle him. "I did," I say, my voice muffled as our mouths bump together. "Nonna thought it might also come in handy when I need to get home. Or maybe to Detroit now and again."

He smiles and snakes his arms around my waist, pulling me close. "Why?" he asks. "What's in Detroit?"

If Dr. Paula's theory is right, if we are the product of the things we say yes to, then a few months ago, I was basically the product of fear. Fear of new things, fear of new people, fear of new experiences, but mostly fear of getting hurt. And even if Dr. Paula's advice wasn't 100 percent solid, I have to admit that it led me to this place, to this person I've become. Who I am becoming. And also to this other person who's standing here with me. I have no guarantee that I won't eventually get hurt. But even so, I think he might be worth it.

If that's what it means to be a product of yes, then I think I can be on board with that. At least most of the time.

"So, you ready for this?" Miles asks. "Ready to *commence* the next chapter?"

I smile and twine my hands behind his neck, threading my fingers together. "Yes," I say.

Unabashedly, unequivocally, *yes.*

ACKNOWLEDGMENTS

You know how there are a hundred adages about "behind every great book . . ." and "it takes a village," etc. etc.? In my experience, every one of them is true. It looks like magic, but this book is the result of so many people working so very hard.

To the entire team at Alloy Entertainment and Random House Children's Books: thank you for your insights, your vision, and your patience. Thanks especially to Wendy Loggia, Viana Siniscalchi, Sara Shandler, and Josh Bank. I know it's not actually magic, but you sure make it look like it.

I wouldn't be where I am today without Amy Tipton's tenacity and steadfast belief. And I wouldn't be where I'm headed without Elizabeth Bewley's enthusiasm and guidance. Thank you both, truly.

One of the things no one told me about becoming an author is that eventually my heroes would become some of my dear friends. "Thanks" doesn't begin to express the debt of gratitude I owe to two such friends, Kara Thomas and Courtney Summers, but I suppose it's a start. Without you, I'd certainly have thrown in the towel ages ago. Also, so much love to Leila Austin, Alexis Bass, Somaiya Daud, Laurie Devore, Debra Driza, Sarah Enni, Maurene Goo, Kristin Halbrook, Kate Hart, Kody Keplinger, Michelle Krys, Stephanie Kuehn, Amy Lukavics, Samantha Mabry, Phoebe North, Veronica Roth, Steph Sinkhorn, and Kaitlin Ward. There are not enough table-flipping or Kool-Aid Man gifs on the entire internet to express my gratitude for the ways you've celebrated and commiserated with me over the years. Also, thanks to the LBs past and present. You all are the OGs.

To every English and/or writing teacher I've ever had, thank you for your part in shaping my life in writing. That goes double for MJ Peters. And maybe a special thank-you to the instructor who once told me my "voice would be better suited to YA" way back when. You meant it as a dig because you didn't understand the extraordinary possibilities to be found in YA (it's okay, it happens a lot), but you actually set me on a path of discovery that opened up the world for me. You should know I've never looked back.

To Sarah, Jennifer, Kellie, Lydia, Katie VA, Lindsey (Other), Krystle, Erin, Nancy, Liz, and Veronica: thanks for the accountability, the cheerleading, and all those gentle reminders that I can do hard things. I certainly won the friendship lottery.

To my family: Mom & Nick, Tyler & Erin, Bob & Judy, you are all simply the best.

Sam, this book would look so very different (by that I mean would not exist) without your support and encouragement. Thank you times a million.

And finally, Carly, Calvin, and Caroline: you are everything. Love you, mean it.